Also in the *SPECIAL AGENTS* series:

*Coming Soon:*

# SPECIAL AGENTS

SPECIAL AGENTS

# FINAL SHOT

## sam hutton

With special thanks to Allan Frewin Jones

Special thanks also to Ashley Jones,
Commercial Manager of the Wimbledon Museum

HarperCollins *Children's Books*

First published in Great Britain by Collins 2003
HarperCollins *Children's Books* is a division of HarperCollins*Publishers* Ltd
77-85 Fulham Palace Road, Hammersmith, London W6 8JB

The HarperCollins *Children's Books* website address is
www.harpercollinschildrensbooks.co.uk

2

ISBN 0 00 714844 5

Text and series concept © Working Partners Limited 2003
Chapter illustrations by Tim Stevens

Printed and bound in England by Clays Ltd, St Ives plc

# Prologue

Night.

02:37

South London, SW9.

The room was small and filthy. Neglected. Long abandoned. It smelled bad. Beyond the grimy window, the rooftops of nearby buildings gleamed black from the rain. The roads and pavements were shiny and wet and empty. A freight train rumbled in the distance.

The room was in darkness. There was one chair. One small, broken table. Nothing else.

A figure sat hunched over a laptop computer. The weak, greenish light from the screen glowed on a pale face with feverish eyes. A dry tongue licked dry lips.

Fingers tapped at the keyboard and words scrolled out on the screen.

```
SHADOW:   I hear you are good at what you
          do. Is that true?
```

The poised hands trembled. Cold sweat ran. A heart was beating fast and hard.
Words began to appear on the screen.

```
SPIDER:   What service do you require?
SHADOW:   I want you to hurt someone. What
          kind of things do you do?
SPIDER:   I work to order. What are your
          requirements?
SHADOW:   I want him to suffer.
SPIDER:   Do you want elimination?
```

Shadow stared at that last line of type. Uneasy. Hesitant.

```
          Elimination.
```

Sweat dripped on to the keyboard. Breath came rapidly in small, hard gasps. A fist clenched in a tight chest.

SPIDER:   Do you want this person dead?

The hunched figure was shaken from its stupor. Fingers began to type, slowly, deliberately.

SHADOW:   I want him humiliated. I want him crushed. I want him finished.

There was a short pause. Then:

SPIDER:   Understood. We need to agree the fee and the method of payment. And I will need full details of the target.
SHADOW:   Not yet. We can discuss all these things when the time comes. I just need to know I can rely on you if you are needed.

Shadow didn't see the need to tell Spider everything at this stage. If Shadow's plans worked out, then Spider would not be needed. Spider was just a fall-back position, in case something went wrong.

Words scrolled rapidly across the screen.

SPIDER:   Unauthorised user detected. Disconnecting now.

1

Shadow stared at the screen. Eyes blank.

SHADOW: What do you mean? Are you still there?

There was no response.

'Damn!' Shadow's face contorted with anger. 'Damn you!' Then the urgency of the situation seemed to hit. Someone was monitoring their conversation. Breath hissed. The head turned sharply and the eyes stared back at the open doorway.

Someone was out there.

Someone was coming.

✪

Danny Bell crouched low over a bank of electronic equipment in the back of the Mobile Surveillance Unit. He was wearing a lightweight headset. He glanced up at monitor screens and digital displays. His fingers moved rapidly over the keyboard of a laptop computer. He was absolutely concentrated on the task in hand. The e-conversation between Spider and Shadow was on-screen.

Two men sat with him in the back of the van. A third was driving them through the rain-wet streets of Stockwell, SW9. All three police officers were older and more experienced than Danny, but on a job like this, they waited on Danny's instructions.

'OK. I've still got them,' he said. 'It's fine. It's cool.' He grinned. 'Keep talking, my friends, just keep talking.' He glanced around at his companions. 'We're close, boys.' He held up a hand; finger and thumb a fraction apart. 'We're *this* close. Hold on to your hats. Lee! Sharp right here.'

The driver responded instantly and the MSU cornered at speed. Bracing themselves against the side of the van, the two officers in the back looked at one another. Being called 'boys' by a eighteen-year-old trainee was a new experience for both of them, but they understood that the young black American knew his stuff when it came to the expensive technology that filled the van. As far as this high-speed chase through the night was concerned, Danny was in control.

Danny was from Chicago. He had come to London with his father under an FBI Witness Protection Scheme. Hiding from the Mob. Scary stuff. But right now, Danny had other things to think about. Right now he was working for the British police.

Police Investigation Command had been tracking the hit man called Spider for months. A lethal assassin, he was famous for killing his victims with a single, clean shot and disappearing instantly without a trace.

Tonight's mission was the closest they had come to nailing him.

In the tangle of streets, Danny's electronic map was proving difficult to follow.

'Is there a right turn coming up?' he asked Lee.

'Yes,' came the reply through his headset. 'It's coming up now.'

'Take it. What does it look like out there?'

'We're in an estate of some kind. A housing estate. It looks pretty grim. I don't think anyone lives here. I think it's being knocked down.'

One of the officers leaned over Danny's shoulder. 'Are you sure this is right?'

Danny tapped keys and watched green and red lights flickering on the digital map. 'Yes.'

The MSU cruised slowly through the semi-derelict housing estate.

The hairs stood up on the back of Danny's neck. 'We're right on top of him,' he whispered. His eyes still fixed on the monitors, he reached out and picked up two oblong signalling bugs. The devices were made of metal, which gleamed dully in the dim light inside the van.

'Ken, Adam – take these. I need you outside so I can pinpoint the location of our friend.' Danny activated the devices. Red lights began to pulse on and off.

The two officers grabbed the bugs and opened the back door of the van. It was no longer raining, but their feet splashed on the wet road as they stepped down. They walked in opposite directions, spreading the signal. The van crawled on, its engine barely turning over.

Danny heard Lee's voice in his headset. 'How accurately can you pinpoint him with this gear?'

Danny grinned. 'I can tell you what room he's in. I can tell you which way he's facing and what colour shirt he's got on. OK, stop the van.'

Danny took the headset off. He carried the laptop to the open back of the van. He pointed to the long dark bulk of the nearest building. Brick-built. Five storeys high, its front striped by grey balconies.

'He's in there,' Danny called to the two officers.

Lee appeared around the side of the van. 'And the colour of his shirt?'

Danny smiled. 'Give me five minutes.' He looked again at the display screen. 'Uh-oh!'

Lee's voice was sharp. 'What?'

'The signal's gone. They've disconnected.'

Detective Inspector Lee Mason took command. There were only two possible exits from the long block of flats. Both needed to be covered. Thirty seconds after the electronic signal had vanished, Danny and

Adam were at the left-hand exit. Lee and Ken were racing towards the other.

'I'll take the first floor,' Adam ordered. 'You take the second. Yell if you find anyone. Don't take chances.'

Danny nodded. He ran up the dark zigzag of concrete stairs. The electricity in the block of flats had been switched off long ago, and the only light came from the orange gleam of street lamps on the road outside. The whole place smelled of damp and decay. Graffiti trailed across the plaster walls in incongruously bright colours.

He came to the long, narrow balcony. There were five doors. He unhooked the torch from his belt and sent a cone of white light along the rubbish-strewn walkway.

He wasn't armed. PIC officers seldom carried weapons. Besides, it wasn't Spider they were expecting to find. It was his latest client. Somewhere in this block, was a man who knew how to get in contact with the hit man. If they could lay their hands on him, they'd be one step nearer to closing Spider down for good.

Danny pushed at the first door. It swung open. He scanned inside with the torch. Wallpaper peeled off the walls. Danny had been a field agent for some months now, but he still hadn't got used to the way his blood chilled at moments like this. He guessed that people never got used to that feeling of hidden danger.

'You get used to it, boy, you get dead,' he whispered under his breath. It was fear that kept the senses alert. He moved into a room. Nothing there. He stepped back into the hall and continued to search the flat. Another empty room, then a narrow galley with a dirt-smeared sink under the window.

Danny flicked the beam of light over the mess that covered the kitchen floor. A pair of bead-bright eyes peered at him from a dark corner. He heard furtive scratching sounds. Rats. A hairy back sped through the rubbish, quick as a bullet. It made him jump. He shivered and backed out of the kitchen.

'Nice rodents,' he breathed. 'I'm out of here.'

The night air was chill after the stale atmosphere of the flat.

Danny's communicator buzzed in his jacket pocket. He took it out. 'Yuh?'

'Are you OK?' It was Lee.

'Oh, just fine,' said Danny. 'There's rats in here the size of buffaloes, but apart from that, I'm having a great time. You?'

'Nothing yet. Be careful.'

'Yeah, Mom, I'll be careful.' Danny disconnected and pocketed the communicator.

The door to the second flat was half open. He

nudged it wide with his foot, listening for rats. He wished his fellow trainee, Alex Cox, was there with him right then. Alex was a physical kind of guy. Alex would know how to deal with rats.

'Rats are OK,' Danny whispered to himself. 'Rats are cute and cuddly.' He stepped cautiously along the hallway. He came into a small, filthy room.

There was one chair. One small, broken table. Nothing else. The hairs on the back of his neck prickled again. His skin crawled. There was something about this room. Something bad. He could sense it. His torch beam crept across the bare floor and up the wall.

Someone had pinned photographs to the wall. Lots of photographs. Danny swallowed. There was something wrong about this. Something sick. He turned a full circle, the circle of light from his torch raking the walls. Every centimetre of space had been covered in photographs of the same young man. His face stared out from the walls over and over and over again.

Most of the pictures were like surveillance shots – long-distance zoom-lens stuff – but there were also a few that seemed to have been cut from magazines or from newspapers.

Danny swallowed hard. A sick mind had been at

work here. In every single one of those dozens and dozens of photographs, the young man's eyes had been sliced out.

# Chapter One

It was a warm afternoon in the middle of June. The sun shone down out of a clear blue sky. The previous night's rain clouds had been blown away. The place was buzzing with lunch-time crowds, strolling through the arcades, wandering in and out of the shops, pausing to watch the street performers: escape artists, jugglers, a fire-breather. A typical Sunday in Covent Garden.

At Ponti's restaurant, an attractive young woman with short, blonde hair approached the self-service counter. The young man serving had already noticed her. She had the kind of face that got noticed. Her friend had taken a table out on the forecourt. She had long, black hair, drawn severely off her face into a ponytail. There was a holdall by her feet bearing the Royal Ballet School logo.

Both girls were slender and their movements held the sort of poise that was born, not learned. The assistant assumed that they were dancers taking a break from rehearsals at the Royal Opera House. He was only half right.

He smiled as the blonde girl approached, but she didn't seem to notice. She gazed along the rows of tempting cakes and pastries. He saw that she had sad eyes. He got the impression that her thoughts were elsewhere.

'Cheer up,' he said to her. 'It may never happen.'

Surprised, Maddie Cooper looked at him. She smiled.

'That's better,' he said cheerfully. 'Can we tempt you with anything?'

'One cinnamon and one almond Danish, please.'

She paid and walked out to the sunlit table.

The black-haired girl had the *Sunday Times* colour supplement open. She looked up as Maddie placed a plate in front of her.

'What did he say?' Laura Petrie asked. 'Did he come on to you?'

Maddie shook her head. She sat down. 'He said,

17

cheer up, it may never happen.' She gave a short laugh. 'If only he knew.'

Laura's face clouded with concern.

'I'm OK,' Maddie said. 'I shouldn't have said anything. You don't have to worry about me.'

'You always say that,' Laura reminded her. She frowned. 'I can never tell what you're really thinking.'

Maddie gazed steadily at her. 'You want to know what I'm thinking?' She took a deep breath. 'OK. I'm thinking I really miss my mum.'

'I'm so sorry, Maddie.'

One night, eleven months ago, Maddie's whole life had been ripped apart in a deadly hail of bullets. Her policeman father had been crippled in the attack. Maddie had been seriously injured. Her mother had been killed.

It had been a revenge attack. Superintendent Jack Cooper had been the prime target – payback for the arrest of a major player in the London underworld. The Cooper family were left bleeding on Floral Street, outside the Royal Opera House where, just a short while earlier, Maddie had been performing in *Swan Lake*. It was her first time on stage – and her last. She recovered from her injuries, but her dancing career was over.

'I shouldn't have asked you to come along to the rehearsals,' Laura said. 'It's just reminded you of everything, hasn't it?'

'Reminded me?' Maddie said softly. 'Oh, Laura – I don't need to be *reminded*. I live with it every day. But I've moved on, you know? I have a new life now. It's not the life that I expected, it's not what I dreamed of for all those years studying ballet at White Lodge – but it's a *real* life, and I'm happy with it. Truly, I am.'

'If you're sure.'

'I am. Now, what did that article say again?'

'You weren't even listening.'

'I am now.' Maddie nodded towards the magazine. 'Come on – what was it about?'

Laura grinned. 'It's a big spread about the hot new tennis stars.' She lifted the magazine and turned it face-outwards to her friend. Laura's eyes glowed. 'Look at him, Maddie. Isn't he the most gorgeous thing you've ever seen in your entire life?'

Maddie looked at the photograph. It was of a young man with short, light-brown hair and a pleasant, boyish face. Above the photograph was a headline. She read it out loud.

'"Will Anderson. Tomorrow's champion or yesterday's news?"' She looked at Laura. 'What does that mean?'

'You know what the press is like – set 'em up and knock 'em down,' Laura said, her face clouding. 'Will's been a bit off-form recently, that's all. Everyone was going on about how brilliant he was last year – and now they're ready to write him off. He was in the semifinals at the American Open last summer, and he very nearly beat Yuri Ulyanov. Do you remember? Will played like an absolute angel.'

'I was in hospital,' Maddie reminded her.

Laura winced. 'Oops. Sorry. My big mouth.'

'That's OK,' Maddie said. 'Anyway, I don't really follow tennis that closely. To tell you the truth, I've never even *heard* of him.'

'You're hopeless!' Laura said, taking the magazine back. 'You'll know all about him when he wins Wimbledon. He's being sponsored by a big Internet sportswear company. They're called Moonrunner. His face is going to be absolutely everywhere. Is that great or what?'

Maddie laughed. 'If you say so.'

'He's not had it easy, you know,' Laura went on, searching through the article. 'Yes, here we are. His parents were both killed in a car crash three years ago. His father was his coach up until then. When his father died, his older brother, James, took over coaching him.

There's a quote here by their mother's sister.' Laura began to read aloud. '"We are very proud of Will and we follow all his achievements with enormous pleasure. Despite the fact that there is only a four year gap between them, James has been like a father to Will. The two boys are inseparable."'

'Is James as good-looking as Will?' Maddie asked with a grin. 'Perhaps we could set up a double date, seeing how you have the hots for Will so badly.'

'I've never seen a picture of James,' Laura said. 'I don't know what he looks like.' Her eyes narrowed as she realised she was being teased. 'Oh! Very funny, Maddie. Ha, ha.'

Maddie laughed. 'I bet you have pictures of him stuck up over your bed.'

'I do not!' Laura said. 'Well, only two.' She turned the page and frowned. 'I really hate the way these reporters put people down. A person is entitled to go off the boil a bit. My guess is he's just saving himself for Wimbledon. Listen to this: "Questions are being asked as to whether Will is still hungry enough to keep his competitive edge, now that he is about to become a media icon. He will not be the first young hopeful to take his eye off the ball at the prospect of all that instant wealth and fame. Will Anderson needs to remain focused on the job in hand and not to spend his time partying when he should be practising."' She looked up at Maddie. 'You'd think they'd want to encourage him. They're quick enough to complain when the great British hope gets knocked out in the first round!'

'Calm down,' Maddie said. 'Anyone would think you were his girlfriend.'

Laura shrugged. 'I wish!' She gave Maddie a look of mock exasperation, then burst out laughing. 'As if! Enough of my fantasies – how's work going? You've hardly told me anything about it.'

'It's good, thanks,' replied Maddie.

'It must be weird, working for your own father,' Laura said. 'Still, I suppose there must be an upside – like, you can goof off whenever you like.'

'Don't you believe it,' Maddie said. 'Dad treats me exactly the same way he treats everyone else. We agreed that right from the start.'

Laura looked thoughtfully at her. 'Is office work really your thing, Maddie? I mean, I know you're making the best of it, but isn't it a bit dull?'

Maddie smiled. 'It's not all office work,' she said. 'I get let out every now and then.'

Laura leaned forward eagerly. 'Like, on special assignments?'

Maddie gave a brief shake of her head. 'You know I can't tell you.'

'Oh, yes, I forgot.' Laura grinned. 'It's all top secret. Harriet the Spy hits London!'

'It's not top secret,' Maddie objected. 'But it is confidential.'

'Don't worry,' said Laura. 'I know how much it means to you. But just you wait, the moment I get cast as Giselle, you'll be the last person to know!'

Maddie smiled and carried on eating her Danish. First thing tomorrow morning, she would be attending the weekly PIC briefing. She wondered what new assignment her father would have lined up for her. She hoped she would be teamed up with Alex and Danny again. Laura was right – office work could be dull, but a hundred hours of paperwork were worth it for one day out on the streets.

# Chapter Two

Monday morning. The rush hour.

The packed Underground train hissed to a halt at Tottenham Court Road. The doors slid open. Maddie joined the stream of people heading upwards to the exits. She felt positive and focused, pleased to be going back to work after the weekend.

She had known that attending Laura's rehearsal would be difficult. It was the first time since the shooting that she had felt able to visit her old White Lodge friends, now students at the Royal Ballet Upper School. She was just relieved she had something to take her mind off the inevitable envy she had felt, seeing them on stage.

Maddie came up to street level at the intersection of Tottenham Court Road and Oxford Street. The great, white tower of the Centrepoint building pierced the sky above her. The crossroads was busy with traffic. Red buses. Black cabs. People hurrying to work. Maddie stood still for a moment, breathing in the energy around her.

She crossed the road and made her way over the plaza to the main entrance. The glass doors slid open and she walked through. As the doors closed behind her, a hushed quietness descended.

A familiar figure was leaning on the reception desk, chatting to the uniformed security guard. It was Alex. He was in his bike leathers. He had arrived at Centrepoint on his beloved Ducati. He was nineteen years old, a Hendon trainee cherry-picked by Maddie's father. Light-brown hair hung over his piercing hazel eyes. His body was fit and powerful. Alex was a good colleague and an invaluable friend – as Maddie had already learned in their few months working together. He turned to smile at her as she flashed her security tag to the guard.

The two colleagues passed through the metal security arch beside the desk and headed for the lifts. Steel doors opened and they stepped inside.

'How was your weekend?' Alex asked.

Maddie briefly told him of her trip to the Royal Opera House.

'I don't suppose that was easy, was it?' he said sympathetically. He knew Maddie's history.

Maddie gave a rueful smile. 'You could say that,' she admitted. 'But I'm glad I did it. Like Gran would say, it's all part of the healing process.'

The lift swept them smoothly to the uppermost floors of Centrepoint. The top four floors were already a hive of activity. It was here that Police Investigation Command – PIC – had its national headquarters, and it was from here that Chief Superintendent Jack Cooper coordinated the operations that spread far beyond the boundaries of the British Isles.

'I wonder if Danny will be in,' Maddie said. Danny Bell had been a rare visitor to PIC Control over the past few weeks. He was on special assignment. He was spending most of his time in the MSU.

The lift doors opened. Maddie felt the familiar shiver of excited anticipation as she stepped into Control. It was a long, open-plan office, brightly lit and full of activity. The hand-picked officers of PIC sat at large tables equipped with the latest computer technology, or stood beside printers at the side of the room, talking in low tones. Large digital screens flickered on the walls.

Jackie Saunders, the Chief Communications Officer, sat at her desk, speaking fluent Japanese into her headset. She acknowledged Maddie and Alex with a brief wave as they passed her.

They spotted Danny straight away. He was at his work station, frowning intently at the screen and typing rapidly.

'Hi, there, stranger,' Alex said.

Danny looked up at them. Maddie thought he looked unusually tense and distracted.

'Hi, guys,' he said tersely.

'Is something wrong?' Alex asked. 'You look like you've seen a ghost.'

Danny stared at his two colleagues. 'A ghost would have been better,' he said.

'What happened?' Maddie asked. She knew that Danny had been out in the MSU on a special assignment over the weekend.

'It'll be in the report,' Danny said abruptly. He glanced at his watch. 'I've got ten minutes to finish it. You'll know everything then.'

Maddie and Alex glanced at each other. Alex gave a small shrug and they moved away. This was so out of character for Danny that it was obvious something had seriously disturbed him.

A voice came over the intercom. 'Alpha Watch Personnel to the briefing room in ten minutes, please.' It was the voice of Tara Moon, Chief Superintendent Cooper's personal assistant.

'I'll get out of this gear and see you in there,' Alex said to Maddie.

She nodded distractedly, her mind still on Danny.

What could have happened over the weekend to affect him so badly?

❂

Jack Cooper moved his wheelchair into position behind the desk in the oval briefing room. He had been in his office long before Maddie had arrived. Following the murder of his wife and the injuries that had crippled him for life, he had thrown himself totally into his work. A deserved promotion had put him in charge of PIC, a unique, specialist arm of the Metropolitan Police, answerable only to the Home Secretary and the Prime Minister.

Tara Moon stood at his side as the officers of Alpha Watch began to file in and take their places. She was twenty-four years old. She had short red hair and fierce green eyes. It was her job to act as chauffeur and personal assistant to the Chief Superintendent – a job she handled with steely confidence.

Maddie came into the room with notepad and pen. She sat down quietly at the long table, giving her father an affectionate look to which he responded with a brief nod. Following the accident, Jack Cooper had felt worried about her. She had been devastated to learn that her dancing career was over before it had even begun. But a new career suggested itself when Maddie asked to be shown around PIC Control on her sixteenth birthday. In spite of Jack Cooper's misgivings about bringing his daughter into the potentially violent world in which he worked, Maddie was hooked. She persuaded her father to let her spend a year at PIC Control, working as part of his team, before returning to her education.

The last couple of officers entered and found their places.

The weekly briefing began.

⊗

Maddie made notes as the various officers gave their reports. Much of it concerned operations she wasn't directly involved with, but Chief Superintendent Cooper believed that his team should have an understanding of all aspects of PIC work.

Maddie tried to concentrate on an update on arms smuggling, but her attention and her eyes kept wandering over to where Danny was sitting. He was hunched over, reading from a print-out. Frowning. Preoccupied.

The officer finished his report.

Now it was Danny's turn to take centre stage. He walked over to take his place at the lectern.

'Three months ago,' he began, 'we started to hear whispers that the Internet was being used by a hired assassin to arrange and coordinate contract killings. To date, there have been three murders which we think are directly linked to this person. He or she goes by the name of Spider and they operate from London. That's all we know for sure.'

Maddie made rapid notes. All this was new to her, although it didn't surprise her that criminals had started to use the World Wide Web for their own ends.

Danny continued with his report. 'A week ago, we got lucky. We monitored a cyber-conversation between Spider and a potential client. The client calls himself Shadow. He contacted Spider from somewhere in SW9. They agreed to make contact again this weekend to talk business.'

Danny then detailed the events of that Saturday

night: the MSU speeding through the darkened streets; the derelict council estate; the foul-smelling stairway and the rubbish-strewn walkway that had led him to that room.

'Lights please, Tara,' he said. Tara moved over to the door and dimmed the lights. 'We missed Shadow by about five minutes, but we found the place he was operating from.' Danny licked dry lips. 'We took some pictures.' He tapped a computer keyboard on the lectern and digitised photographs appeared on individual screens in front of each officer.

The first picture was of a small, dirty room. There was a table and a chair. The floor was bare boards. The window, a black hole into the night. The flare of the flashbulb showed that the walls were covered with photographs, pinned chaotically.

'I've seen some creepy stuff before,' said Danny, 'but this is something else. Take a look at this.'

He tapped a key. Another picture appeared, showing a close-up of one wall.

A murmur ran around the room.

There were maybe ten photographs in the picture. Ten photographs of a handsome young man. In six of the photographs, the eyes had been neatly sliced out as if with a sharp knife. In the other four, it looked as though a cigarette had been applied to the paper, completely burning out the eye sockets.

Danny flicked through a couple more photos.

As before – scores of photographs of a young man with his eyes missing.

Danny took a deep breath. 'I guess we can assume we're looking at Spider's next victim.'

Maddie was staring at her screen in amazement. The sight of all of those mutilated photographs was horrible enough – but there was worse.

'I know who that is,' Maddie said.

All eyes turned to her.

She swallowed, looking away from the screen. 'He's a tennis player. His name is Will Anderson.'

# Chapter Three

The burned-out eye sockets of Will Anderson stared out from the monitor screens in the hushed PIC briefing room. There had been nods of recognition from some of the other officers following Maddie's announcement. But all eyes were now focused on Maddie.

'Go on, Maddie.' Jack Cooper's voice was a low growl in the tense silence.

'I don't know much else about him,' Maddie said. 'There was an article on him in yesterday's *Sunday Times* supplement. He's English; seventeen years old. He is expected to do well at Wimbledon this year. That's about it.'

'Thank you, Maddie,' Jack Cooper said. He made a

note on the pad in front of him and looked up at Danny again. 'Danny – finish your report, please.'

'I'm just about done,' said Danny. He flashed a series of similar photographs up on the monitor. An obsessive repetition of the same handsome, boyish face, each and every one blinded by knife or fire.

'We got forensic in, but they came up empty,' Danny explained. 'There's no water or electricity in the flat, so I don't think that Shadow lives there. He's just been using it as a safe house – a place for his picture gallery, and somewhere private to make contact with Spider.'

He tapped the keyboard again and the disfigured faces on the monitors faded to grey.

The lights came up.

'OK,' Danny said, glancing at his notes. 'What does this tell us about Shadow? My guess is that he doesn't live alone. If he did, he'd have put that freak show up somewhere more comfortable. So, he shares a home with at least one other person. A wife, maybe. Girlfriend? Flatmates? Mom and Pop? Your guess is as good as mine. This is the closest we've gotten to Spider in three months, and I am *really* ticked off that this sick lunatic got away from us.'

Danny gathered his notes and went back to his seat.

'The way Shadow defaced those photographs

suggests he doesn't like Mr Anderson very much,' Jack Cooper said dryly. 'Most of them were shots of him going about his daily business. Shadow must have been following him around with a zoom lens.'

'Maybe Shadow is a stalker,' Danny suggested. 'One of those people who obsesses about celebrities. They can get pretty weird and twisted.'

'Or maybe Shadow knows Anderson personally,' said Jack Cooper. 'We need to speak to this young man – see if we can gather a few clues as to Shadow's identity.'

Tara Moon lifted her head. 'I think we need to play this one very carefully,' she said. 'If Shadow *is* someone Will Anderson knows, an official police presence might frighten him off. And that puts us back to square one with Spider as well.'

'Agreed,' Jack Cooper said. He looked around the room. 'Any suggestions?'

'Someone could pose as a reporter,' Alex suggested. 'Anderson will think it's just another pre-Wimbledon interview. That should give us open access to him and the people around him.'

'That's good,' Jack Cooper said.

Maddie frowned. 'Excuse me,' she said, 'but shouldn't we warn him about this?' She looked around the room. 'Surely we should tell him that some crazy person has put out a contract on him? At least then he'll be on his guard.'

Section leader Ken Lo, who had been in the MSU with Danny, spoke up. 'I disagree. Anderson has to behave normally. That's not going to happen if we tell him he's in the cross wires of a professional hit man. We have to focus on tracking Shadow down. Then we use Shadow to nail Spider.'

'But in the meantime, Will Anderson could be killed,' Maddie said. 'Even if we don't tell him, can't we at least give him some kind of protection?'

Jack Cooper shook his head. 'We don't have the resources to offer twenty-four-hour cover, Maddie. You know that.'

Maddie lapsed into an uneasy silence. She understood her father's reasoning, but it still seemed a dreadful thing to leave Will Anderson on his own with this threat hanging over him.

Alex waved his pen. 'I don't necessarily think it would be a waste of resources to have someone keeping an eye on Anderson,' he said. 'I really think Shadow knows him. The eye-gouging stuff – that's too personal. It's nasty. It's someone who hates him. I don't think you get to hate someone that intensely from a distance.'

'What do you have in mind?' asked Jack Cooper.

'Instead of just sending someone to interview Anderson, why don't we try to organise something that would last a bit longer?'

'A profile for a magazine,' Maddie suggested. 'A day-by-day account of Will's preparations for Wimbledon.' Her eyes lit up as she looked at her father. 'If you're worried about it being a waste of time, why not send someone who's not that important?' She gave her father a hopeful smile. 'Someone who won't be missed too much for a few days.'

Jack Cooper looked steadily at his daughter. He knew exactly what she was getting at. She wanted to be that someone.

Maddie was on tenterhooks. Would he go for it? She knew she could do it. She was already picturing herself in the role of an eager young journalist working for a national magazine: *marie claire*, maybe, or a Sunday broadsheet.

It took Chief Superintendent Jack Cooper exactly five seconds to crush Maddie's budding hopes.

'Alex? I'm giving this to you,' he said. 'Track Anderson down. Tell him you're a freelance writer and that you want to do a big article. Be convincing. Tell him you'd like to spend a few days with him – that should give you time to get to know him and the people around him.'

Alex nodded. 'I'm on it, Boss.'

Jack Cooper looked around the room. His voice was gruff. 'And while Alex is out there winning a Pulitzer for journalism, the rest of us are going to be on double shifts until Shadow is tracked down. This is our number one priority, people. Get out there and work this city. That's all. Dismissed.'

There was a rustle of papers and the scrape of chairs as the room began to clear.

'Maddie?' She turned at her father's voice. 'I'd like a word, please.'

Jack Cooper waited until they were alone.

He looked closely at his daughter, his grey eyes clear and steady on her face. 'Do you understand why I gave this assignment to Alex?' he asked quietly.

She nodded. 'Because if anything happened, Alex would handle it better than me,' she said calmly. 'And you're right – he would.'

There was a pause, then her father's voice came again, barely above a whisper. 'There is another reason.'

'Yes, Dad. I know.' She smiled and gave him a mock salute. 'Trainee Officer Cooper requesting permission to go and do some work, sir,' she said.

Her father gave a gruff laugh. 'Get out of here, Maddie.'

As she headed back to her work station, her smile faded. She knew exactly what her father's other reason was. If there was a gunman out there, the very last person in the world that Jack Cooper was prepared to put between Will Anderson and a bullet was his own daughter. She understood perfectly. She just hoped that one day she would be given the chance to prove that she could look after herself – to prove herself the equal of any officer in PIC. She knew she had it in her. She knew she would make a good operative.

Maddie sat down at her work station and turned to her in-tray. She frowned. There was always the paperwork to keep her busy. With a sigh, she reached for the topmost file, her ambitions temporarily on hold. Her time would come.

# Chapter four

A private tennis club in Roehampton.

One week before the Wimbledon Tournament.

Alex watched Will Anderson through a mesh of wire fencing. He wasn't a big tennis fan, but he knew enough to admire the range of shots Will used, and the speed with which the ball was fired back over the net by the young tennis star. He could see why the newspapers were hyping Will as the next big thing.

After a while, Will raised his racket to call a break. He trotted to the side of the court and picked up a towel. He wiped his face. He was sweating and breathing heavily.

Alex's eyes narrowed thoughtfully. Maybe Will was

not quite as super-fit as he seemed at first glance. A true champion would have strolled through that short training session without raising a serious sweat.

'Hi, there,' Alex called.

Will Anderson looked up at him. The final piece of the high-profile jigsaw fell into place. He had the kind of face that Alex could easily imagine gazing out from billboards and magazines. He was a marketing department's dream come true.

'Hello.' Will stood up. 'Are you Alex?'

Alex nodded. Will called to his training partner. 'Give me half an hour.'

The two men walked together into the clubhouse.

'James told me to expect you,' Will said. 'What magazine are you working for again?'

'I'm freelance,' Alex said. 'But I've got a lot of interest from *Newsweek* and there's a good chance of international syndication if I can deliver the goods.'

Will smiled. 'And what goods would those be?'

'The inside story,' Alex said, smiling back. 'The real Will Anderson. An in-depth study with plenty of glamour and scandal. The ups and downs of your life so far. The lowdown on all your secret supermodel girlfriends. That kind of thing.'

Will shook his head. 'Sorry,' he said. 'James's training

schedule doesn't include time for supermodel girlfriends. It's boring, I know, but this close to Wimbledon, all I really do is train and sleep. And I split up with my girlfriend four months ago – and she wasn't a supermodel.'

'I've already come up with a title for the article,' Alex persisted. '"The Will To Win." What do you think?'

Will pulled a face. Alex laughed. 'I'm still working on it,' he said. He was about to make some comment about Will's rise to fame when they were interrupted.

An inner door opened and a man came out into the reception area. James Anderson was taller and thinner than his brother. He was good-looking, with the same dark-brown eyes, but his angular face lacked the boyish quality that made Will's face so universally popular, and so instantly recognisable, Alex thought.

James strode across and shook Alex by the hand, smiling warmly. Alex wondered if he was so welcoming to every stranger that came to talk to his brother.

'Nice to meet you,' James said. He looked at Will. 'Everything OK?'

'Yes, fine,' Will said. 'Alex wants to know about my love life.'

James grinned at Alex, raising his eyebrows in mock exasperation. 'No great secrets there, I'm afraid,' he said. 'Will is in love with tennis.'

'Nice one,' Alex said. 'I'll remember that for the article.'

'How long were you wanting to spend with us, Alex?' James asked. He pulled out a mobile phone and looked questioningly at Alex, his thumb poised over the keypad.

'Three or four days would be good,' Alex said. 'If that's OK with you.'

'No problem,' James said, hitting a speed-dial number on the mobile. 'I'll just call Rufus and let him know that you've arrived.'

○

'So who's Rufus?' Maddie asked.

Maddie, Alex and Danny were in the rooftop canteen at PIC Control. The long picture windows gave them a breathtaking panorama of the London skyline, shimmering under a clear blue sky.

Alex was filling his colleagues in on his first meeting with the Anderson brothers.

'Rufus Hawk is Will's big new sponsor,' Alex explained. 'He runs Moonrunner.'

'The sportswear firm?' Danny said. 'Big bucks, then, huh?'

Alex nodded. 'It seems like it,' he said. 'According to

James, Hawk has plenty of publicity stunts lined up. There's an official launch party on Thursday. On a boat on the Thames.' Alex smiled. 'I'm invited, and I can bring a friend or two along, if I like. Rufus wants the boat packed out with as many people as possible – preferably A-list celebs, but I guess you'll do,' he added with a grin. 'I think he's trying to kick-start Will-mania.' He looked at them. 'Any takers?'

'Yeah, why not?' Danny said. 'I'm always up for free food and drink.'

'I'll pass,' Maddie said. 'I can't see myself as a tennis groupie. Tell us some more about Will Anderson? Did he say anything that gave you any leads on who Shadow might be?'

Alex shook his head. 'Not so far,' he said. 'But I should have a better idea of the kind of people he hangs around with by the end of the week. There is an ex-girlfriend. Sonia Palmer. They were together for six months. Will called it off last year. He said she was taking up too much of his time.'

'Sounds pretty ruthless,' Maddie said.

'He is when it comes to tennis,' Alex admitted.

'So, what's he really like?' Maddie asked.

'It's difficult to tell from one meeting with him, but he seems like a nice bloke.' Alex looked thoughtful. 'If

I really was writing an article about him, I think I'd focus on his relationship with his brother. There's a heavy bond between them. It can't be easy, having your own brother as your coach, but they seem to get along just fine. James is obsessed with Will's career. He was telling me that his ambition is to see Will achieve a top ten world ranking by the end of Wimbledon.' He shrugged. 'I'm not convinced, though,' he said. 'I watched Will training. I don't think he's up to it. He didn't seem match-fit to me.'

'A lot of people are going to be disappointed if he crashes out in the first couple of rounds,' Maddie said. 'My friend Laura, for one, will be devastated.'

Alex nodded thoughtfully. 'And she won't be the only one,' he said. 'Rufus Hawk is going to be feeling pretty sick if his goose doesn't lay the golden egg. There's a lot of money riding on that guy's shoulders.'

Maddie wondered what it must be like to be loaded down with all those expectations. The pressure to succeed must be unrelenting. And as if that wasn't enough, the young athlete also had a secret enemy, someone who hated him enough to set a contract killer on him.

All things considered, Maddie didn't envy Will Anderson one little bit.

45

✪

Maddie lived with her father and her gran in an apartment block that overlooked the northern end of Regent's Park. The low, tree-fringed buildings and enclosures of London Zoo were visible from their living-room windows. That evening, a warm breeze was drifting in from the south. The windows were open, leading out on to a narrow balcony crowded with potted plants.

Gran was kneeling on a plastic-covered cushion on the balcony, prodding fiercely at some compost in a heavy terracotta pot. A tray of densely flowering seedlings lay beside her.

Maddie was sitting up on the windowsill with her bare feet on the back of the couch. She was watching a bright-yellow scooter weave through the traffic in the street below, while she listened to Laura on the telephone. Laura had managed to get hold of a ticket for the first day of Wimbledon, and couldn't wait to share her triumph with Maddie.

'And if I'm really lucky,' Laura was saying, 'I might get to watch Will play. If I do, I'm definitely going to get his autograph. That guy is going places!'

Maddie laughed. 'I should have told Alex to get you a ticket to the launch party,' she said. 'You'd have loved it.'

'What launch party?' Laura asked. 'What tickets? What are you talking about?'

'One of the guys I work with has been invited along to some kind of a do with Will Anderson on the Thames tomorrow night,' Maddie explained. 'Will has just signed a deal with a big new sponsor and—'

'I know!' Laura interrupted. 'With Moonrunner. I've got a pair of their sweatpants. Hang on, Maddie – are you saying you know someone who's going to meet Will, and you didn't bother telling me?'

'Sorry,' said Maddie. 'I didn't think. I was invited too, but it didn't appeal to me.'

Maddie grinned to herself as her friend let out an exasperated snort.

'Now you listen to me, Maddie,' Laura said firmly. 'You've got to go to that party, and you've got to get Will's autograph for me – *and* a photo, and any other free stuff they happen to be giving out, even if it "doesn't appeal" to you! Come on, you know I'd do the same for you!'

'OK, OK,' Maddie said. 'I'll go to the party. I'll get his autograph – but it'll be a total nightmare, so you're going to owe me big time for this, got me?'

'Maddie Cooper, I love you!'

'Oh, shut up!'

Maddie sighed. That was the last thing she needed – to be crammed on a river boat for an evening with dozens of news-hungry paparazzi in some crazed media feeding frenzy.

Still, she thought, it served her right for telling Laura about Will Anderson's launch party in the first place. She should have known how mad Laura was about Will – in fact, Maddie thought, she should count herself lucky that Laura hadn't insisted on coming along as well, invite or no invite! She just hoped that the evening wouldn't be too tedious. Meeting Will would be OK, but Maddie suspected she and the guys would just be lost in a melee of journalists and ego-boosters, revolving like over-eager satellites around the big star.

# Chapter Five

The river cruiser was a blaze of lights as it slid slowly along the Thames. The main cabin ran almost the whole length of the boat, and was lined with broad windows. Every inch of space was filled with young journalists and Moonrunner hangers-on, dressed with artful casualness in top-of-the-range designer sportswear. The noise was intense. A DJ was set up behind a pair of decks in one corner and music was being blasted out through 500-watt speakers. Finger food was piled high on tables that ran along one side of the room. There was nowhere to sit. There was no space to dance. No space even to breathe.

From Maddie's point of view, there was nothing to

do except try to avoid being trodden on by the people forcing their way from one part of the boat to another, and to do her best to lip-read what Danny and Alex were saying to her.

'Great party,' Danny yelled in her ear.

Maddie looked at him. Was he kidding? Someone jogged her elbow and she narrowly avoided spilling her drink.

Alex put his mouth close to Maddie's ear. 'I'm going to go check on Will,' he bellowed.

She nodded. 'I need some fresh air,' she shouted. She gestured towards the prow of the boat. Danny gave her the thumbs up as he pushed into the mass of people and quickly disappeared

Maddie fought her way towards the doors that opened out on to the triangular front deck. Cool air blew through her hair. There were only a few people out here, chatting together under the canvas canopy. It had become quite dark since she had come on board with Alex and Danny. On either side of the river, the Thames-side buildings were lit up with thousands of tiny orange and white lights. Further off and higher up, blocks of bright white pinpricks were all that could be seen of the tall towers of the City. Ahead of them, the ornate Gothic pillars of Albert Bridge were uplit dramatically with soft, white light. Its supports were hung with chains of illuminated globes, like strings of pearls.

Maddie gazed down into the river, watching the prow of the boat as it cut through the black water, folding it back in swathes of white foam. Feeling suddenly cold, she turned, bumping into someone standing just behind her with his back to her.

'Oops. Sorry,' she said. He turned and smiled.

'No problem,' he said. He was tall, with a pleasant, angular face. 'Enjoying yourself?'

She smiled wryly. 'Not much,' she admitted. 'It's a bit of a crush in there.'

He laughed. 'Tell me about it,' he said. 'It's like feeding time at the zoo. Everyone wants a piece of Will tonight. He's going to be shattered by the end of it.'

'He must enjoy it, though,' Maddie said. 'He wouldn't go along with it otherwise.' She gave a small shrug. 'I can't see what all the fuss is about, to be honest. He might be a great tennis player, but he's not *that* special, is he?'

The tall young man smiled. 'Some people seem to think so.' He squared his shoulders. 'I suppose I'd better get back down there,' he said. 'Have a good evening.'

'You too.'

The man pressed his way through the doors and was soon absorbed by the crowd. Moments later, a familiar face appeared at the glass and Danny came out.

'It's heating up in there,' he said, fanning himself with one of Moonrunner's promotional flyers. 'Was that James Anderson I saw you talking to?'

Maddie stared at him. Her hand came up over her mouth. 'Oh, no – it wasn't, was it?'

'I'm pretty sure it was,' Danny said. 'Alex pointed him out to me earlier on.' He grinned. 'Why, what did you say to him?'

Maddie grimaced in embarrassment. She explained. Danny thought it was hilarious.

'I've got to go and apologise,' Maddie said. 'And then I think I'll throw myself in the river.'

Danny followed her back into the crowded cabin. James Anderson was nowhere to be seen. The music had been turned down a little, and it was almost possible to hold a normal conversation. They found Alex. He was with a thin, pale-faced man with curly, ginger hair and red-tinted shades. The man was wearing an immaculately tailored suit, which flattered his gawky frame and spoke volumes about his bank balance. His hands dripped with jewellery. Maddie's instant impression was that the man valued his own opinion as much as his personal appearance.

'It's been great to meet you, but I have to go,' the man was saying. He was shaking Alex's hand, but his eyes flicked round the room, scanning for the next person to see and be seen with. 'I mustn't neglect my guests. People to see, deals to make.' He moved off, his face fixed in an artificial smile. It made Maddie think of a hungry shark.

'Where's he from?' she asked Alex. 'The planet Ego?'

'Probably,' Alex said. 'That was Rufus Hawk.'

'The boss of Moonrunner?' Danny said. 'There you go, Maddie – you've just met a multimillionaire. What did you think?'

'No comment,' Maddie said.

'He's only a multimillionaire on paper,' Alex commented. 'If Moonrunner doesn't really start performing, most of his money could vanish overnight.'

'From what I've heard,' Danny said, 'he's got his fingers in other pies, too. He's into property development of some sort, if I remember correctly – or he was a few years ago.'

'Well, I wouldn't have anything to do with him,' Maddie said. 'He's got shifty eyes.'

'Shifty eyes and a big bank balance,' said Danny. 'This sponsorship deal is going to keep Will Anderson in glucose drinks for a long time to come.'

'Where *is* Will?' Maddie asked. 'I haven't seen him yet – I'm supposed to be getting his autograph.'

'Follow me,' Alex said. 'I'll introduce you.'

'And I need to find James,' Maddie added.

'Why?'

'Don't ask.'

It didn't take Alex long to track Will down. He was standing just beyond an inner door, at the top of a flight of polished wooden stairs leading to the lower deck. He was holding a half-full tumbler, and studying the clear liquid intently.

'Hello, Will,' Alex said. 'How's it going?'

Will started and looked up. He seemed to relax slightly when he recognised Alex, throwing him a tired, haunted look. 'I hate all this,' he said. 'I feel like I'm in a goldfish bowl.' He looked at Maddie. 'Now I know why Rufus picked a boat for his launch party – it's so I can't escape.' He laughed and rolled his eyes.

Maddie laughed too. 'I hate to do this to you,' she said, 'but I'd really like your autograph. It's for a friend. She'll kill me if I don't get it.' She winced. 'I don't suppose you have any signed pictures of yourself?'

'Stacks of them,' Will said. 'I'm sick of looking at my own face – and the big advertising campaign hasn't even started.' He smiled crookedly at Maddie. 'If Rufus gets his way, my dumb face is going to be everywhere. Can you believe it?' He laughed again. 'All I want to do is play tennis – how did I let myself in for all this?'

'It's all part of the fame trail,' Alex said. 'You'd better get used to it, Will.'

'Tell me about it,' Will sighed.

He seemed to be genuinely uncomfortable with the whole setup. Maddie found herself liking him for his reluctance to cash in on his popularity. But that only made her feel worse about what she'd said to James. She was even more determined to find him and apologise.

✪

The hot, noisy evening continued. Danny mingled among the crowds, eavesdropping on the confident, commercially-minded conversations going on in every corner of the boat. It seemed as though everyone wanted a slice of Will Anderson. Danny found himself wondering whether there was enough of Will to go round.

Alex kept close to Will, secretly screening everyone who approached him – watching for some word or glance that might hint that Shadow was one of the people at the party.

James and Rufus Hawk appeared.

'What are you doing here?' Rufus asked Will. 'You should be out there, working the main room. I can't do everything myself.'

'I'm tired,' Will said. 'I needed a break.'

'You'll get a break when the show is over,' Rufus said. 'Right now I need you to go and change.' He looked at James. 'Both of you. OK? The clothes are laid out in that cabin back there. Come through as soon as you're ready. I'll go grab the mike. I've got an announcement to make.'

Rufus Hawk waded back into the crowd.

'We have to go and change into Moonrunner Sportswear stuff,' Will explained to Alex. His voice sounded flat with tiredness, and there were dark circles beneath his eyes. 'Then there's a big photo shoot, and then we can all go home.'

The brothers were about to walk down the stairs to the small cabins at the rear of the boat, when Maddie appeared.

'Excuse me, James?' she said. 'Could I have a quick word?'

'I'll catch up with you,' James said to Will. He looked at Maddie. 'Hello again.'

Maddie's face was anxious. She beckoned James over to a relatively quiet corner at the back of the cabin.

James was smiling.

'I feel like a total idiot,' Maddie said. 'I had no idea who you were when I spoke to you earlier.'

James laughed. 'No problem,' he said. 'I've heard worse. And Will would probably have agreed with you anyway.'

Maddie smiled back, relieved that James had not taken offence. She couldn't help liking both the Anderson brothers, who seemed surprisingly unaffected by the media circus that was going on around them.

At the other end of the main cabin, the DJ silenced the music and Rufus Hawk stepped out from behind the decks, holding a microphone.

'Ladies and gentlemen, if I could have your attention for a few minutes.' The buzz of conversation slowly subsided. 'Thank you. First of all, I'd like to thank you all for coming aboard tonight. We all know why we're here – to celebrate the sponsorship deal between Moonrunner Sportswear and one of Britain's greatest young athletes – Will Anderson. Will and James will be here soon, to show you some of Moonrunner's latest collection. But meanwhile, I have another important announcement to make...'

Maddie and James turned to listen.

'What's he going to announce?' Maddie asked James.

'I have no idea,' James said. 'But I should go and change.' He made to follow where Will had disappeared downstairs, but hesitated to listen to Rufus's announcement.

'The sponsorship deal with Moonrunner Sportswear signifies a major turning point in Will's career,' Rufus continued. 'He will now be in a position to launch himself into the very highest ranks of world tennis. And with this in mind, I have arranged for one of the world's foremost tennis coaches to join Will's team. You'll all know his name – he's coached some of the best players on the international scene. I'm talking about none other than Lars Johansson. He will be flying in from Denmark tomorrow to start Will on a new training regime in the run-up to Wimbledon. And with Lars on our team, I'm more convinced than ever that Will Anderson's name is going to be inscribed on the Challenge Cup at the end of this year's Wimbledon fortnight!' A brief murmuring filled the cabin, followed by loud applause.

Maddie looked at James. He was staring across the

room, his face a stunned blank. He wasn't clapping. It was brutally obvious that he had known nothing of this. He was no longer going to be Will's coach. But what a way to find out!

People standing nearby turned to look at James. Maddie saw the effort it took for him to crank up a smile. He began to clap. Maddie was impressed by his composure – Rufus Hawk's surprise announcement must have devastated him.

✪

Below decks, Alex watched as Will passed through a door at the end of the short corridor. Instinctively, he followed. The door closed quietly behind him, cutting them both off from the rest of the boat. Alex was standing in a cramped lobby, with three doors leading off.

Will was in an open doorway to one side. He flicked a light switch. The small cabin through the doorway remained dark.

'Problem?' asked Alex.

'The bulb's gone,' he said. 'Great. We'll have to get changed in the dark.' He looked over Alex's shoulder to the door which led to the corridor. 'Where's James?'

'I think Maddie wanted a quick word with him,' said Alex.

Will turned. 'Can I tell you something strictly off the record, Alex?' he said. His voice was weary.

Alex nodded.

'There's something wrong with me,' Will said in a low voice. He looked down at his hands. Alex thought he sounded desperate. 'I don't know what it is. It's driving me crazy. I'm tired all the time. My reflexes are blown. Unless I can pull myself out of this slump pretty quickly, I'm going to crash and burn at Wimbledon.'

He shrugged and walked into the darkened cabin.

Alex followed him in.

The door slammed behind them. The room went black. Alex turned with snake-like reflexes. Something was wrong.

He heard Will grunt behind him. There were scuffling sounds in the pitch darkness. They had been ambushed! Alex lunged for the door to the lobby – he needed some light. He careered into something. Hands grabbed for him. He drove a hard punch at stomach level. There was a gasp. More hands clutched at him, trying to pin his arms. He shrugged off the attack and snatched at the door handle.

He wrenched the door open a sliver. He saw a startled face in the bright thread of light. A heavy face. Stubble. Razor-cut hair. Bulging eyes.

A foot crashed into the door, wrenching it out of Alex's hands. Two men launched themselves at Alex, forcing him to the floor. His ears were ringing as his head struck the boards. Red light exploded behind his eyes. Dazed, he knew he only had seconds to act.

He heard a voice, quiet and controlled. 'Don't hurt them.'

A knee pressed into his back. His arms were pulled backwards. His attackers had been lurking in the dark cabin – their eyes had adjusted to the gloom. They had all the advantages.

There was plenty of fight left in Alex, but if he started a pitched battle in there, Will might get hurt. He didn't want to risk that.

Moments later some kind of slender tape was slipped around Alex's wrists and pulled tight. Any hope of getting free was gone. He was hauled to his feet. A cloth bag was thrown over his head and drawn closed around his neck. He was bumped and jostled out of the cabin and pushed to the left, towards the small lower deck at the stern of the boat.

He felt cool moving air. He vaguely heard applause coming from above him in the main cabin. He struggled against the hands that were holding him.

'Cut that out,' said the cold voice. 'Trust me. No

one's going to get hurt. But you've got to do exactly what you're told.'

A voice called softly from somewhere below them. 'OK. I'm ready. Let them down. Gently, now.' Alex could hear the sound of water lapping against the side of the cruiser.

It was obvious to him what was happening.

Will and Alex were about to be taken off the river cruiser on to another boat.

They were being kidnapped.

# Chapter Six

Rufus Hawk's announcement had caused a lot of impressed speculation in the crowded cabin. Voices buzzed as the surprise news of Lars Johansson's appointment was discussed.

'I'm sorry, ladies and gentlemen,' Rufus called above the noise. 'I don't know what's keeping Will and James. I'm sure they'll be here any moment.'

At the back of the cabin, Maddie looked at James. His jaw was set, but he was doing his best to mask his shock. Maddie felt desperately sorry for him.

'I'll just go and see what's keeping them,' Rufus Hawk said into the mike. He obviously didn't even know that James had been there to hear the bad news.

Rufus Hawk made his way along the length of the cabin, heading for the stairs.

James's eyes blazed. He made a move as if to head Hawk off. Maddie put her hand on James's arm. He paused. Hawk left the cabin.

Maddie looked sympathetically at James. 'You didn't know anything about that, did you?' she said.

James's eyes narrowed. 'He's some piece of work, isn't he?' he whispered. 'He didn't waste any time taking over. The ink's hardly dry on the contract.'

'But surely he can't make decisions like that without consulting you?' Maddie protested.

James looked at her. 'I think he just did,' he said.

Maddie's response was cut off by a shout from the back of the cabin.

'They aren't there!' It was Rufus Hawk. He was standing in the doorway, a look of panic on his face. 'Will and James aren't on the boat. Something's happened to them. We have to call the police!'

A stunned silence came over the party people.

James thrust forwards. He caught Hawk by the lapels. 'What the hell are you talking about?' he said. 'What's going on here?'

Hawk stared at him as though he couldn't believe his eyes. 'I... I thought...' he babbled. 'You... and...Will...'

From the other side of the cabin, Danny reacted instantly. He slipped past the two men, down the stairs and pelted along the narrow corridor to the lobby at the stern of the boat. A cabin door was open. The cabin was in darkness. It took Danny about thirty seconds to check that there was no one in this or the other cabin. He pushed through the third door in the lobby and came out on to the open deck.

He ran to the stern. A spreading wake of white water gleamed on the river. Where the two white ripples met, Danny could see a fist of darkness. A boat. A small boat, moving rapidly downriver, kicking up white foam.

The motorboat sped into the darkness under Westminster Bridge. It vanished.

Danny hung on to the rail, staring out over the river. He had seen Will heading for the back of the boat. He had seen Alex follow.

He slipped his mobile phone out of an inside pocket. He pressed a speed-dial number. He held the phone to his ear.

The line opened to PIC Control.

'It's Danny,' he said into the phone. 'We have a problem.' His eyes narrowed. 'I think the term is *man overboard*!'

✖

Alex sat in the back of the speeding boat, his hands bound behind him, his head covered by the cloth hood. The wind buffeted him as the boat cut through the water. He was alert to his very fingertips, poised and ready to take advantage of anything that might help him to get Will and himself out of this situation.

Not that there was much chance of that right now. The kidnappers weren't speaking to each other, but judging from the sound of their movements in the small boat, Alex guessed there must be at least four of them.

His brain was racing. The kidnappers must have climbed aboard and hidden themselves in that small cabin some time after dark. They had disabled the light to give themselves an extra advantage. Then they had waited – which meant they must have known Will and James would be going in there at some point in the evening.

It was obvious that both the Anderson brothers were the targets, not Alex. Will was the one worth kidnapping – he was the one who could command a heavy ransom. James was probably only meant to be taken along to stop him sounding the alarm.

Alex smiled grimly. Except that these guys hadn't kidnapped James – they had taken a PIC officer by mistake. Big mistake, once Alex got free.

Judging by the whip of the wind, Alex guessed that

they were moving at high speed. Not wise to make a move yet. He would have to stay cool for the time being.

All he could do was to listen – and wait.

❂

The cruiser had slowed and was heading towards the nearest mooring place. There was confusion on board. Everyone was aware that something had gone badly wrong. Two people had vanished. Not both the Anderson brothers – as Rufus Hawk had first thought – but Will Anderson and a journalist called Alex Cox.

Danny and Maddie were careful to conceal Alex's real identity for the time being. They wanted to wait for orders before they revealed who Alex really was – or who they were, for that matter.

They pulled away from the crowds, retreating to the corridor below deck where they could talk in private. Danny still had an open line to PIC Control.

'We're just coming in to Lambeth Pier,' he said into his mobile. 'Are the River Police on the case yet? Good. No, there was no sign of violence. They must have taken Alex by surprise. I saw the boat in the distance – it was really moving. Yes, heading east under Westminster Bridge. I'll keep you in the loop.' He pocketed the phone and looked at Maddie.

'What's going to happen when they find out they haven't got James?' she asked.

'Alex can look after himself,' Danny said. 'I hope.'

'Do you think Spider took them?' said Maddie.

Danny's voice was uneasy. 'Maybe.'

'Who else could it have been?' Maddie was afraid that Will and Alex had been taken by the unknown assassin.

'I don't know,' Danny said. 'But don't start assuming the worst, OK?' He frowned, remembering all those pictures of Will Anderson with his eyes taken out. Shadow was a psycho. If he'd handed Will over to a cold-blooded killer like Spider, then things could have just got deadly serious.

'I'd better go and check that James is OK,' Maddie said. 'He must be worried sick.'

'Don't tell him *anything*,' Danny warned her. 'The less he knows, the better, right now.'

Maddie nodded.

There was chaos and confusion in the main cabin. Rufus Hawk seemed to be holding some kind of impromptu press conference. He was surrounded by a scrum of people with tape machines and cameras. Maddie scanned the room for James. She couldn't see him.

Then she heard Hawk say something that caught her attention.

'I blame myself for this,' he was telling the reporters. 'I should never have kept it to myself, but I didn't take it seriously. I'll never forgive myself if anything happens to Will.'

She pushed in closer, wanting to hear what Hawk had to say.

'The truth is,' Hawk began, his voice sounding strained, 'I've been receiving phone calls threatening Will's safety for several weeks now. I didn't tell him – or anyone. I thought it was all nonsense.' He took a breath. 'I was wrong,' he said. 'I now believe that Will Anderson has been kidnapped, and that a large ransom will be demanded for his safe return.'

Maddie stared at him in shocked disbelief. He had received kidnap threats and he'd done nothing. And now, thanks to his arrogance and stupidity, Will Anderson and Alex were in the hands of a professional hit man. For all Maddie knew, Spider might already have executed his contract.

Will and Alex could already be dead.

# Chapter Seven

The small motorboat moored. Alex was pulled up out of the boat. Firmly, but not roughly. He was made to walk forwards, his arms held by two men. They walked over solid, level ground. He could hear other footsteps. Will and his captors. There was a pause. Alex heard the scrape of what sounded like a large gate being opened. Beyond the gate the ground was rough and uneven. They entered a building. Doors hissed closed. The floor pressed against his feet. They were in a lift. Going up. The movement stopped, and Alex heard the doors slide open. A nudge against his shoulder blade told him to walk out.

The men only spoke in subdued whispers. They gave

no instructions to their hostages – making their intentions known by guiding with a hand on the shoulder. A door was opened. Their footsteps echoed loudly in a large empty room. Another door, then Alex was pressed down on to the hard concrete floor. His ankles were bound. There was the sound of footsteps moving away. A door closed.

Then there was only silence.

'Will?'

'Yes.'

'Are you OK?'

'Yes. I think so. You?'

'Yes.'

There was a fearful catch in Will's voice. 'I can't believe this is really happening. I keep thinking I'm going to wake up.'

'Try to keep calm. There's nothing we can do right now.'

'Who are these people? What do they want with us?'

Alex didn't answer straight away. He was thinking hard.

'I think they plan on making some quick money,' he said at last. 'My guess is they think I'm James. They think they've grabbed the Anderson brothers. They're going to demand a big ransom to give us back.'

Will groaned.

Alex wasn't entirely convinced by his own explanation. If Spider had taken them, then things could get very bad very quickly. But there was no way he was going to tell Will about that.

'Just try to relax, if you can,' Alex said levelly. 'Focus on something positive. Think about how you're going to win Wimbledon once we get out of here.'

Will gave a short, bitter laugh. Alex knew he had to try to stop Will from brooding on what might happen to them. He asked him questions about tennis, training, his life – question after question – keeping Will's mind occupied.

Gradually, as time passed, Will's answers became slower. Eventually, uncomfortable and afraid as he must be, his voice faded away. Alex guessed that he must have fallen asleep. Good.

Alex worked on his bonds. He had flexed his wrists while they were tying him up. That gave him some slack to play with. He worked his arms, twisting and pulling. Gradually, minute by slow minute, he felt the ties loosening. He rested, gathering his strength. He concentrated all his power and determination and made a final great effort to slide his hands apart. He gave a gasp of relief as his hands came free. He pulled the hood off his head. It was dark. The room was clean and absolutely bare. The night sky showed through broad, uncovered windows. Will was slumped in a corner, his head down.

Anything that might have been useful to Alex had been taken from his pockets and dumped in the river – knife, keys, mobile phone. Everything. He was thankful he hadn't had his PIC ID on him. Alex turned his attention to the plastic cord that was wound around his ankles. The knots weren't difficult to undo. He sat for a short time, massaging life back into his feet – pins and needles – he stood up and walked across to the windows.

They were high up. Very high. He found himself looking down at the curve of the river and beyond to the night-lit southern suburbs of the city. The sky was starry. The darkness had reduced London to a confusion of black shapes outlined by pinpoint patterns of lights. Alex frowned, trying to get his bearings. He guessed they were somewhere in Docklands. The smell of paint and fresh-cut wood suggested that they were being held in a newly built tower block. Not an office block – the room they were in was too small. A residential block, then. Luxury flats overlooking the Thames.

Alex moved to the door. He pressed the side of his head to the panel and listened intently, holding his breath. There was nothing. No sound. Either the kidnappers were no longer within earshot, or they were keeping deathly quiet.

He walked quietly over to where Will was huddled. Crouching down, Alex gently loosened the hood and drew it off his head. Will muttered something under his breath, but he didn't wake up. Alex worked carefully and silently on Will's bonds. They came loose. Without waking, Will slipped sideways into a more comfortable position on the floor. Alex stood up, looking down at him with a furrowed brow. He would let him sleep until dawn.

And then what?

Alex had no idea.

✪

There were a series of digital clocks on the wall of the main office in PIC Control. They were set with split-second accuracy for time zones throughout the world. The display set to UK time showed 04:07. The room was brightly lit and full of urgent activity. A dozen officers had been summoned to Control. No one had slept. They were all surviving on coffee and adrenaline. One of their colleagues was missing, and no one was going to take time out until he had been found. Field agents and officers were out in the night, searching for clues, reporting back, waiting for new orders.

Jack Cooper was coordinating the search personally. Maddie and Danny were at his side. Danny wanted to be out there on the streets, but Cooper needed him at Control. He had been on the boat – he had information that would help to build up a picture of exactly what had happened.

Detective Inspector Susan Baxendale appeared at the head of the conference table beside Jack Cooper. She had been interviewing Rufus Hawk.

'Well?' Cooper snapped.

'He's sticking to the same story,' the DI reported. 'He says he received four or five threatening phone calls over the past two weeks. He says the caller demanded one hundred thousand pounds, and said that if he didn't get it, something bad would happen to Will Anderson. Hawk says he didn't contact the police because he figured it was just some harmless crank.'

'Stupid jerk,' breathed Danny.

Jack Cooper lifted his hand. 'Do the calls check out?' he asked.

Susan Baxendale nodded. 'I've already done a search. All the calls were made from a public phone in

Docklands. We've got people on stakeout over there, but I'm not hopeful. If this is about ransom money, they're not going to be so dumb as to make calls from a number they'll know we'll have traced.'

Jack Cooper nodded. He glanced at his watch. 'There's been no word for six hours.' He looked around the table. 'So, what do we think, people? Are we expecting a ransom demand?'

Maddie stared at her father. She understood only too well what he was getting at. Were Alex and Will being held hostage, or had they been taken to their deaths?

'It's too soon to assume the worst,' said Tara Moon. 'Alex will know how to keep things under control.'

'If it's Spider, why didn't he just do the job on the boat?' Danny said carefully. 'Why take them away?'

'That's exactly what I'm wondering,' said Cooper.

'Could Shadow have taken them himself?' Maddie suggested. She was so tired she could hardly think straight, and keeping track of two faceless killers seemed like an impossible task, even for her father and his team.

'It's possible,' DI Baxendale agreed. 'Shadow could have taken them to some pre-arranged safe place. He leaves them there, then Spider moves in and does the job without compromising his own safety.'

Maddie shivered. It all sounded so clinical, the way they were talking – but the reality behind it was the lives or deaths of two men.

'Spider is an assassin, isn't he?' she said slowly, thinking aloud. 'He gets paid to kill people. But Rufus Hawk said the person on the phone was demanding money.' She looked around the table. 'It doesn't make sense. A contract killing and a kidnapping for ransom are totally different things.'

'Maddie's right,' Danny said. 'Something's screwy.'

'Let's think about this,' said Jack Cooper. 'Are we convinced that the man making the calls to Rufus Hawk was Shadow? The person who wants Will Anderson dead?'

'It has to be,' Tara said. 'Who else could it be?'

Jack Cooper frowned. 'If that's the case, where does Spider fit in? We know Spider's a professional assassin. He kills people. He doesn't do kidnapping.'

'Maybe he's there for backup in case something goes wrong,' DI Baxendale suggested. 'If the deal blows up in Shadow's face, Spider would make sure there weren't any witnesses.'

'What about those photos of Will with his eyes taken out?' said Danny. 'If Shadow is only interested in money, what was going on with those pictures?' He shook his head. 'I still think we're way off the mark. There's something else going on here – I just wish I could figure out what.'

Jack Cooper's voice was subdued but determined. 'Meanwhile, we keep thinking and we keep searching,' he said. He looked at Baxendale. 'Have you had Hawk taken home?'

DI Baxendale nodded. 'Jakes and Peterson are with him. They'll make contact if anything happens.'

Maddie looked at her father. 'Is there anything else we can do?'

Jack Cooper gazed at her with his steady grey eyes. 'Yes,' he said. 'We wait. And we try to work out who is behind all this – Spider, or Shadow, whoever that might be.'

✪

Alex awoke from a shallow sleep. He had spent most of the night silently prowling their prison. Weighing up their options. Will's safety was his priority. Will had to be got out of this situation in one piece – nothing else mattered.

Exhaustion had finally made Alex sit down. He had slept without meaning to.

The sky was less dark now. A grainy, grey light was filtering into the room. Dawn could not be far off. He stood up and went to the window. A strip of light brightened the sky behind the buildings that stretched away to the east. The sun was about to rise.

Alex knelt by Will's side.

He shook him.

Will's eyes opened. He looked confused at first – then his face clouded.

Alex gave a rueful smile. 'No, it wasn't all a dream,' he said. 'Sorry. How are you feeling?'

'Stiff,' Will said. He sat up. 'Has anything happened?'

Alex shook his head. 'All quiet so far.'

'I'm thirsty,' Will complained. 'They should give us water, surely?'

Alex put his hand on Will's shoulder. 'I want you to listen very carefully to me,' he said. 'There's something you need to know. I'm not a journalist. I'm a police officer.'

Will stared at him. 'You're *what*?'

Alex looked at him. How much could Will take? How much of the truth did it make sense for Alex to tell him? Enough for him to realise that the situation was potentially dangerous, but not so much as to scare the life out of him.

'I was assigned to keep watch on you,' Alex said. 'We thought you might need protection.'

Will's eyes blazed. 'You mean you knew that this was going to happen but you didn't *tell* me?'

'No, not exactly,' Alex said. 'We weren't expecting this.'

Will scrambled awkwardly to his feet. 'You should have warned me!' he shouted. 'What's going to happen when those men find out you're with the police?' His voice shook with anger and fear. 'I'll tell you what's going to happen – they're going to panic, and we're going to end up dead!'

# Chapter Eight

'No one's going to end up dead,' Alex said in reply to Will's angry outburst. 'We're going to get out of here in one piece, OK?'

'How?' Will demanded.

'By using our brains,' Alex said. 'And by keeping our cool. Right?'

Will stared at him. When he spoke again, his voice was calm. 'I want to know what's going on here,' he said. 'I want to know everything.'

Alex nodded. It made no sense to keep Will in the dark any more. Things had gone too far for that. He told Will about Spider. He told him about the e-conversation they had monitored. He told him about

Shadow and about the abandoned flat with the photographs. He only left one part out. He didn't tell Will about the eyes. Alex decided that was a detail too far.

Will listened to it all with remarkable calm. Alex watched him, feeling relieved. He needed Will to be in control and not to panic.

Will looked unflinchingly into Alex's eyes. 'So?' he said. 'What happens now?'

'I think it's time to find out what kind of people we're dealing with,' Alex said. 'There were other police officers on the launch. They'll have clamped a security lid down on this whole story. Which means we should still have one big advantage.'

'The men out there still think you're James,' Will said.

Alex nodded.

'Are you good in a fight?' Will asked.

Alex smiled. 'Oh, yes,' he said. 'Very good.' He stepped up to the door and stood for a few seconds, facing the door, psyching himself up for a confrontation with their attackers. He looked over his shoulder. 'Give me plenty of room,' he said.

Will moved back.

Alex raised a fist and hammered on the door. 'Hey!

We need some food in here! We need water! Hey!'

It was like banging a drum. The whole building seemed to echo with the noise. There was no response. Alex tried again, shouting at the top of his voice.

He paused for a moment, thinking. The door opened inwards. There was no point in him trying to kick his way out.

'Are you sure it's locked?' Will asked.

Alex looked round at him, one eyebrow raised. Will shrugged. Alex reached for the lock. He turned the knob. He pulled. The door opened so suddenly that Alex nearly ended up on the floor. Will let out a breath of surprised laughter.

The hallway beyond was empty. Alex moved cautiously out into the deserted space, poised to go into action if necessary. Will followed him. There were other doors leading off the hallway. Another empty room. A bathroom. A kitchen. There was no sign of the kidnappers. Thankfully the water supply was connected. Both men drank thirstily from the chrome mixer tap at the sink.

Alex opened the front door of the flat. He stepped into a wide hallway. Directly ahead of them, behind sleek mirrored doors, stood the lift.

'We'll use the stairs,' Alex said.

There were a lot of stairs. At each crook in the stairway, there was a tall window. London was revealed in the hazy light of dawn. The eastern sky was flecked with yellow. The windows of distant buildings reflected the light. The Thames glistened.

They came at last to the ground floor. Soundlessly, Alex gestured for Will to hold back. He eased though the door into the lobby. Work here was unfinished. Electric cables hung from the walls. The floor was bare cement. White tape crisscrossed the glass doors that led out of the building.

Alex beckoned Will to follow. They edged out into a building site that surrounded the block of flats. Heavy machinery stood idle. The ground was uneven. The area was fenced in by tall plywood panels in rough wooden frames.

They moved across the building site. Alex's mind was racing. What was going on here? Where were the kidnappers? Where was anybody?

They came to the plywood wall. There was a tall pair of gates, sturdy and wooden, with no helpful bars for foot or handholds. They were padlocked and chained from the outside.

'Are you any good at climbing?' Alex asked.

'I'm not great with heights,' Will confessed ruefully.

'OK,' Alex said. 'We'll try something else.'

Alex aimed a series of expert kicks low down on a plywood panel. Bit by bit the board was prised loose from the timber framework. Soon there was enough of a gap for the two of them to squeeze through.

They emerged into a paved area. Trees sprouted from brickwork tubs. There were wrought-iron benches. High railings guarded brand new apartment blocks. They were in one of Docklands most exclusive residential developments. And they were being watched. And barked at.

A woman was standing about twenty metres away, staring warily at them. A sturdy tan-coloured bull terrier was straining on its leash, yapping and snarling – desperate to get loose and attack the dishevelled strangers.

Alex moved towards the woman. The dog went crazy. The woman took a step backwards, dragging the dog after her. 'Don't come any closer!' she shouted. 'I have a mobile phone. I'll call the police.'

'I am the police,' Alex shouted back.

Will came up next to him. 'He is,' he called. 'Honestly.'

'I take self-defence classes,' the woman yelled. 'I'm not afraid of thieving scum like you.' The dog was going ballistic, writhing about like a firecracker on the end of his leash.

'Oh, great,' Alex murmured, glancing at Will. 'She thinks we're muggers.'

He held his hands up towards the woman. 'We surrender, ma'am,' he called. 'There's no need for violence. We won't move, OK? Now, will you please call the police before that dog of yours gets loose and we end up needing rabies shots.'

The woman finally seemed to get the message. She slipped her phone out of her handbag and pressed 999.

✪

The digital display showed 05:27.

Tensions were running high at PIC Control. The regular calls from officers in the field had a deadening monotony: *nothing to report*. It was as if Alex and Will Anderson had just vanished off the face of the earth.

Maddie had been to the washroom more than once, splashing cold water on her face to fight the fatigue brought on by being awake for twenty-seven hours.

Spirits were low. Jack Cooper gave little away, but his short, terse responses to queries and comments made it clear that he was worried. Danny was hunched over his laptop, scanning the Web for some trace of communication between Spider or Shadow. It was better than doing nothing. Idleness just gave his imagination the opportunity to work overtime.

Maddie went back to her work station. She slipped the headset on and waited for the call that would either bring relief or despair. DI Baxendale hurried into the office. All eyes turned to her.

'You should see this,' she said. She leaned over a keyboard and typed rapidly.

The wall monitors came alive. They were tuned to Sky News. A banner at the bottom of the screen blazed the words LIVE EXCLUSIVE.

'This is being broadcast all over the country,' Baxendale said. 'Hawk must be out of his mind.'

The scene was a doorstep in front of an immaculate Georgian townhouse, bathed in white light from high-wattage lamps. The door was open. Rufus Hawk, dressed in another, equally expensive-looking suit, was talking to a crowd of reporters. Flashbulbs went off like strobe lights. Hand-held mikes and boom mikes all pointed towards him.

'I can add very little to the official statement I sent out earlier,' he was saying.

Jack Cooper's eyes blazed. 'He's put out a statement?' he growled. He looked at Susan Baxendale.

'Put me through to Jakes and Peterson. What the hell are they playing at over there? Why have they let him talk to the press?'

'We are still waiting for the kidnappers to make contact,' Rufus Hawk continued. 'But I have decided that I will pay whatever ransom is demanded. Will Anderson's life is in danger, and I will do nothing to jeopardise his safe release.' He raised his arms to fend off a wave of questions. 'I would just like to say this,' he announced. 'Although Will is a client of mine, I also think of him as a friend. And it is as Will's friend that I would like to make this direct appeal to the kidnappers. Please do not harm him. We will comply with whatever demands you make.' He ran his hand through his red hair. 'All I want is for Will to be returned safely and speedily. If the kidnappers have a single spark of decency, they won't prevent Will Anderson from taking part in the Wimbledon tennis tournament – and from claiming his rightful place as this year's men's singles champion.'

Maddie stared at the monitor. 'I don't believe this,' she said. 'Will's life is in danger, and all he can talk about is Wimbledon. Is he crazy or what?'

Danny stood at her side. 'Take a real good look at him, Maddie,' he said. 'Hawk's turning this into one big publicity stunt.'

A phone shrilled. Tara Moon picked up.

'Yes, he's here.' She handed the phone to Jack Cooper. He listened, his face showing nothing. He said a few brief words, then put the phone down.

'Kill that,' he said, nodding towards the monitor. The sound was cut off. All eyes were on him. 'I've just been speaking to Alex Cox,' he said. 'They're safe. And they're free.'

# Chapter Nine

Jack Cooper sat at his desk at PIC Control. Behind him, the broad windows of his office showed the roofscape of the city – the high dome of St Paul's Cathedral, the huge spoked wheel of the London Eye, the Houses of Parliament. The sky was blue and clear. It was mid-afternoon.

Gathered in the Chief Superintendent's office were several section leaders. Alex, Danny and Maddie were also there. They had managed to snatch a few hours sleep before being summoned to the debriefing. The kidnap and bizarre escape of Will Anderson and Alex was the only item on the agenda. Tara Moon was taking notes.

DS Kevin Randal was speaking. 'My people have been right through the building.' He shook his head. 'There are fingerprints all over, from maybe fifty or more sources. I'm having them cross-referenced, but I'm not hopeful. It'll be workmen. This has all the hallmarks of an amateur job gone wrong. A botch-up.'

Jack Cooper looked at Alex. 'Any comments?'

Alex nodded thoughtfully. 'If not for the fact that we know Spider is lurking somewhere out there, I'd say Kevin had it about right.' He tapped his pen on the desktop. 'Things went wrong for them from the moment I opened the door in the cabin and caught sight of one of them. They should have quit then.' He shrugged. 'My guess is that once they'd had time to think things though, they panicked and legged it.'

'Unlocking the door first,' Danny added.

Alex nodded.

Danny frowned. 'So, you don't think this had anything to do with Spider at all?'

'If Spider had been involved,' Alex said, 'Will and I would be floating face down in the Thames right now. I think this whole business was set up by Shadow.' He looked at Danny. 'Remember what he wrote in that conversation you monitored?' Alex flicked through his notes. 'Shadow wrote: *I just need to know I can rely on you if you are needed.* Note the "if". My guess is that Shadow only wanted Spider as backup in case the kidnapping went wrong.'

'And the kidnapping did go wrong,' Maddie said quietly. 'So, what happens next?'

'We follow every possible line of enquiry,' Jack Cooper said. 'Why were Alex and Will Anderson taken to that particular building? Why were they abandoned and left to make their own way out? Why was there no ransom demand? Was Shadow behind it? Was Shadow one of the kidnappers, or did he hire them? If so, from where? We need to put feelers out in all the usual places – find out if anyone has any names to sell. If Shadow recruited the men locally, then someone must know about it.' Jack Cooper looked around the room. 'But remember, our priority is to get Spider off the streets. Don't get sidetracked.'

'What about Will?' Maddie asked.

Jack Cooper smiled grimly. 'He'll get 24/7 protection from now on. We won't be caught napping again.' His voice became a low growl. 'We got lucky – he wasn't hurt. Let's not chance it a second time.'

'I'll get in touch with some of my contacts in the East End,' Danny said. 'If Shadow is nosing around for muscle, they'll know.'

'No, Kevin can deal with that,' Cooper said. 'I have something else in mind for you. I want you to find out all you can about that apartment block. There must be reasons why the kidnappers chose to take Alex and Will there.' He pointed his pen at Danny. 'Find them.'

Jack Cooper pushed his wheelchair away from the desk. 'Meanwhile, Alex and I have somewhere else to go.' He looked across at his assistant. 'Tara? The car, please. Ten minutes.' Tara stood up and left the room.

'Dad?' Maddie asked. 'What about me?'

'DI Baxendale will keep you occupied, Maddie.' Jack Cooper banged his hands down on the arms of his chair. 'OK, meeting over. Let's get moving.'

✪

Six people were gathered in a small room in the Roehampton clubhouse. The room was small and bright. Picture windows looked out over tennis courts, where two white-skirted women were playing in a flood of sunlight. Looking pale and tired, Will was sitting with his back to the windows. James was perched on the arm of his chair, his hand resting protectively on Will's shoulder.

Rufus Hawk was leaning back in the largest armchair. He had a smug, self-satisfied look on his face. The cat that got the cream, Alex thought. And why not? The newspapers and TV news were full of the story of Will's capture and extraordinary escape. Rufus Hawk had made sure of that.

Seated bolt upright on a hard chair next to Hawk was a tall, gaunt man with iron-grey hair and hard, uncompromising eyes. His arms were folded. His face revealed nothing of what he was thinking. His name was Lars Johansson. He had arrived that morning from Denmark.

Jack Cooper was trying to convince Will that he needed round-the-clock protection if he was going to be kept safe. Will hated the idea of police officers dogging his every footstep.

'Excuse me.' Hawk's voice was a purring drawl. 'Might I be permitted to say a word at this point?' All eyes turned towards him. 'You see, Inspector—'

'Chief Superintendent,' Cooper corrected him.

The sportswear mogul waved a hand. 'Whatever.' The muscles along Jack Cooper's jaw bunched. Rufus Hawk was beginning to irritate him. 'The point is,' Hawk continued, 'you're asking the wrong person. You shouldn't be asking Will – you should be asking me. I'm the one who makes all the decisions for Will, now.' He examined his flawless manicured fingernails. 'I might decide to hire a private security firm. I'm not very impressed by the standard of protection you've been offering my client so far.' He looked at Alex. 'No offence, but he could be lying dead in a ditch for all the good you've been.'

Alex bristled, but he knew better than to get into a row with the arrogant millionaire – especially in front of his boss.

'I think valuable lessons have been learned,' Jack Cooper said. He gave Hawk a long, hard look. 'You are perfectly entitled to organise your own security arrangements, Mr Hawk, but we're not going away. A crime has been committed, and we have reason to believe that Mr Anderson is still under threat. As long as that is the case, I'm the one who makes the decisions – not you. I think Mr Anderson needs blanket protection, at least until we have concluded our investigations.'

Hawk smiled coldly at Jack Cooper. 'Don't you think you're overreacting, Inspector – or whatever you call yourself?' he said with calculated disrespect. 'This man – this person who calls himself Shadow – he's made his play and he's failed. I can't see him trying again. The world's media is focused on Will now – who in their right mind would try to harm him under those circumstances?'

'Who says he's in his right mind?' Alex said.

'While we're on the subject of the media,' Jack Cooper put in smoothly, 'I'd strongly recommend that you stop giving interviews to the press, Mr Hawk. It's quite possible that the man who had Will kidnapped is enjoying all the publicity you've given him. It might even convince him to try again.' Cooper's voice lowered to a growl. 'There are people around who'd do harm just for the pleasure of watching the aftereffects.'

Hawk lifted his eyebrows briefly but said nothing.

'Do you think Will's life is in danger?' James said. He gripped his brother's shoulder tightly as he spoke, the knuckles of his hand straining against the skin. Alex was surprised that Will didn't flinch away.

'It's a possibility we have to confront,' said Cooper. 'Shadow has been in contact with a known contract killer. It would be foolish to underestimate the potential danger.'

Rufus Hawk laughed. 'A contract killer? Here? In Roehampton? Please, Inspector, what do you think this is – a movie? All stars get weird phone calls from time to time. It goes with the territory. I'm really not prepared to overreact to satisfy some crank.'

Will had been gazing down at the floor throughout these exchanges. He looked up now and gestured towards Alex. 'If it wasn't for him, I might still be tied up in that place. I could have starved before anyone found me. If I have to have a bodyguard, I want Alex.'

'That man did nothing to prevent you from being kidnapped.' Hawk gave Alex a contemptuous look. 'I can hire the best bodyguards in the country. Just leave it to me.'

Will glared at him. 'Don't I get to make any decisions in my life any more?' he said. He glanced at Johansson and then back to the expressionless face of Hawk. 'Don't you think you've done enough already?'

Hawk breathed deeply. 'We've been over this ten times already,' he said calmly. 'Go and read your contract again, if you're still confused. I have the right to make all executive decisions on matters that directly affect my investment.' He pointed at Will. 'Remember, *you* are my investment. It was my decision that you should have the best trainer that money could buy.' He made an arch of his fingertips and looked steadily at Will over them. 'Anyone would think you didn't want to win.'

'In other words, what you're saying is – take the money and keep your mouth shut,' James said heatedly. 'That was never intended to be the deal.'

Rufus Hawk spread his hands. His heavy gold ring

caught the light. 'How quickly people choose to bite the hand that feeds them,' he said slowly. 'A few months ago you were begging me to take Will on – and now you object to me protecting my investment.' He leaned forward. 'Have you forgotten how much money is at stake here, Anderson?' His eyes were cold. 'I've agreed to keep you on the payroll for the time being, James – don't make me change that contract detail.'

'On the payroll,' James spat. 'What as? Assistant Trainer?' He looked at Johansson. 'What am I supposed to do? Fetch drinks and pick up towels?'

'If it's too demeaning for you, there's an easy alternative,' Hawk said. 'You can quit.' He narrowed his eyes. 'There's the door.'

'No!' Will said. Beads of sweat broke out on his forehead. 'I won't allow that. James stays.' He looked up at his older brother. 'I can't do it without James. I need him with me.'

'And you shall have him with you,' Hawk's voice was suddenly oily. 'I have no quarrel with James. I only want what is best for you, Will. And Lars is the best.' He smiled. 'I just wish you could see that. My only concern is for you – for your career.' He looked from brother to brother. 'Surely, that's what we all want, isn't it?' He raised his eyebrows. 'And it would all be much easier if wounded pride didn't get in the way of common sense.' This was directed towards James. 'Well, I tried. If you want me to break Lars's contract and let you go back to being coached by James, then so be it. I shan't argue with you.' Hawk turned to Will with a glacial stare. 'Is that what you really want?'

Will ran his hands over his face. There was a long silence. 'No,' he murmured. 'That's not what I want. But I can't do my best without James.'

Hawk looked at James. James nodded curtly.

'Excellent,' Hawk said. 'See how easy that was? Now, everyone's happy. Lars can start you off on a new training regime straight away, and hopefully he'll be able to sharpen you up a little. You'd be the first to admit you need it, wouldn't you, Will? You know you've not been performing at your best recently. Lars is going to turn that around. You'll see – before you know it, you'll be out on Centre Court, holding the Challenge Cup and wondering why you made a scene in the first place.'

Alex watched this exchange in grim fascination. He had to admit that Hawk was a smooth operator – slick as oiled glass. He had manipulated that whole exchange like a master, forcing Will into a corner, putting James on the defensive, getting his own way at every turn. Alex had to admire his shrewd manoeuvring, even though he could find nothing to like about the man. One thing was for sure – if Will or James tried to cross Rufus Hawk, they would be in for a very rough ride.

Lars Johansson spoke for the first time. His voice was deep and harsh and crisply accented. 'I cannot do my job properly if Will is to be surrounded at all times by policemen.' His hand chopped the air. 'It is impossible. I will not do it.'

'Alex will keep a low profile, Mr Johansson,' Cooper said. 'He won't get in your way.'

Johansson bent his head in acknowledgement. Hawk shrugged as if he took no interest in the finer details of Will's police protection.

'So, it's decided, then,' said Jack Cooper. 'Alex stays.'

# Chapter Ten

It was midday. Maddie sat hunched in her bedroom, with the curtains closed. She was still in her white towelling dressing gown, curled on a chair with her feet tucked up under her. Her fingers moved over the keyboard of her PC. The screen changed and changed as she moved from one site to another. She was surfing the Net – but she wasn't just passing the time. She was searching for something.

There was a light tapping on her door.

'Come on in,' Maddie called.

Her gran stepped into the room. 'It's very dark in here,' she said. 'Shall I open the curtains for you?'

'Hmm? Oh – yes please.'

The sprightly lady picked her way across the untidy floor. She pulled the curtains wide and sunlight flooded the room.

Maddie blinked.

'There, that's better,' her gran said, cheerfully ignoring the chaos of her granddaughter's bedroom. 'It's a lovely day out. I'm going to the garden centre to pick up some more potting compost.' She leaned over Maddie's shoulder. 'Do you want to come, or are you too busy?'

'I think I'll give it a miss, if that's OK,' Maddie said. 'There are some things I need to get finished.'

Her gran smiled. 'Homework?'

'Sort of.' She looked up into her gran's kindly face. 'I've been asked to compile some data on Will Anderson. I'm just checking the Internet. I'm getting plenty of hits, but it's mostly stuff about the kidnapping, or stats about his career. I was really hoping to find something a bit more interesting.'

Her gran looked at the screen, frowning slightly. 'Why don't you try another search engine?' she suggested. 'Perhaps a UK-based one would be more helpful.' She rested her hand on Maddie's shoulder. 'Don't work too hard.' She shook her head and gave a small laugh. 'I don't know why I bother saying that,' she chuckled. 'You're just like your father – you won't give up until you find what you're looking for.'

Maddie smiled up at her. 'Am I really that much like Dad?'

Her gran nodded. 'You've inherited all your father's stubbornness – but you also have your mother's courage and common sense. It's a good combination.' She leaned forward to lightly kiss Maddie on the top of her head. 'Don't forget to have some lunch, OK?'

'I won't.'

Her gran left the room. A few moments later, Maddie heard the click of the front door. Alone in the apartment, she focused her attention back on the computer screen. She wanted something more than those recent news reports – and something other than a bland list of Will Anderson's accomplishments on the world tennis circuit.

She finally found what she was looking for on a website set up by a fan. A detailed home page appeared on screen. Maddie was impressed. Someone had put a lot of effort into this site. It contained in-depth profiles on a whole host of British tennis players.

Maddie clicked on to the Will Anderson page. There were several photos. Action shots, and portraits. There was also a biography. Maddie leaned closer. This was exactly what she wanted.

Will and James Anderson were born and raised in the leafy south London suburb of Chislehurst. Their mother, Eliza, was a solicitor, and their father, Henry, was a successful businessman, managing a company which sold office stationery. James was four when Will was born. The two boys wanted for nothing as they grew up. Henry Anderson had always been a keen sportsman, and he was quick to spot his sons' potential on the tennis courts at their local club. The two boys were encouraged to enter junior and school-based competitions. At this time, James seemed to be the star of the family, winning several London and South East England championships before a tragic accident brought his budding career to an abrupt halt.

Maddie sat upright. A tragic accident? To James? This was news. Her eyebrows lowered as she leaned forward and continued to read, her fingers tapping the mouse almost unconsciously to scroll the page.

James was eleven years old when the accident happened. Seven-year-old Will had climbed a tree in the garden, and realised he couldn't climb back down again. James was inside the house when he heard Will calling for help. He climbed the tree to rescue his brother, but it seems that a branch broke and both boys fell over the fence into the neighbouring garden. They fell into a large rose bush. Will was knocked out when he hit his head on a paving stone. His brother was more seriously hurt, when the fall damaged his right eye.

Their neighbour, Mrs Marion Greer, came to their aid. She drove the boys straight to hospital.

Will quickly recovered and showed no sign of any serious after-effects following the fall. James was less lucky. He was rushed into surgery with a ruptured eyeball. The surgeons did all that they could, but when the bandages were removed, he was completely blind in his right eye. This was the end of his tennis-playing career — a devastating blow to him and his whole family — and especially to his

brother Will, who felt responsible for the
accident.

Maddie sat back. She let out a long, pent-up breath.
James was half-blind! It was impossible to tell from just
meeting him. Maddie had no difficulty in understanding
how James must have felt when he realised all his
dreams and hopes had been destroyed. Exactly the
same thing had happened to her. The feeling that your
whole life was over. The feeling, almost, that you had
no real reason to carry on living.

She scrolled the page up to a portrait of Will. How
must he have felt? It must have been terrible for him.

Maddie carried on reading. Tragedy seemed to
haunt the Anderson family...

Seven years later, both their parents were
killed in a car crash. Somehow the two boys
recovered from this second blow. Will
carried on with his budding tennis career,
and James overcame his sight disability and
replaced their father to become Will's
coach. In spite of everything, Will kept on
winning. He threw himself into his career and
since then has risen steadily through the

world ranks, with James always at his side.

Maddie gazed out of the window. Deep in thought. Seeing nothing. Just at the moment when it seemed that Will Anderson was poised for the ultimate triumph, Rufus Hawk had casually swept James aside and replaced him with a complete stranger.

On top of that, there was the kidnapping, and the fact that Will was being dogged by an apparent madman. Maddie's eyes narrowed with determination. If PIC couldn't track Shadow down, the luckless family might soon be facing its third and final tragedy: the cold-blooded murder of Will Anderson.

# Chapter Eleven

Danny was busy. He was also bored. He leaned back in his chair, tapping the keyboard at arm's length. He watched the computer screen through half-open eyes. He had spent the entire morning in PIC Control. He was becoming stir-crazy. Offices did that to him. He preferred to be outside. Or in the MSU, listening to the hidden sounds of the city as they sped through the streets.

He yawned and stretched out his legs. His brief was to get some background on the building in which Alex and Will Anderson had been imprisoned. If *imprisoned* was the right word for a couple of guys who were able to get free just by turning a door handle, he thought sceptically.

Danny soon found a useful website. It listed the details of all major construction work in Docklands. He zeroed in on what he needed. The luxury apartment block was called Angel Buildings. The development even had its own website. Danny was impressed by the graphics. The home page had computer-generated visuals of how the building would look once it was finished. The banner heading for Alex's prison was *Angel Buildings – Live like an Angel in the skies above London.*

Danny clicked to get into the site. A white screen appeared with blue print on it.

SITE TEMPORARILY UNAVAILABLE.

Danny frowned. Strange. He tried again. Everything except the home page was locked out. Danny had to make the best of what appeared on the home page. He discovered a couple of things.

The management company was called Redbridge Holdings. To his frustration, Danny could find no other information on this firm. He went back to the Angel Buildings home page. Redbridge was not responsible for actually putting the building up – that was being done by a firm called HCGM Construction.

Danny dug deeper. He used a search engine to track down HCGM Construction. Bullseye! They had an office in London. There was a phone number, an email address, a fax number, contact names. Danny went for the quickest option. He gave the handset of his desk phone a practised slap which sent it cartwheeling off its stand. He caught it deftly in mid-air with one hand and tapped out the number with the other.

Five minutes later, Danny was out of there, his jacket slung over his shoulder as he stood grinning in the descending lift. The phone call had given him the perfect reason to be out on the streets. The CEO of HCGM was visiting a building site only a few blocks away from PIC Control. A guy called Eric Black. Maybe he would be able to shed some light on who actually ran Redbridge Holdings.

The building in Holborn was a mass of scaffolding hung with protective sheets. It looked like the whole place was being gutted. Danny flashed his PIC identity card to gain access. They gave him a hard hat and pointed him towards where Eric Black was standing, deep inside the building, holding up some rolled-up blueprints and talking with the site foreman. Black was stubby and thickset, with a heavy, red face. Danny waited until the brief conference was over.

'Excuse me, Mr Black,' Danny said. 'Do you have a moment or two?'

Black frowned at him. 'No,' he barked. 'I'm busy.'

Danny lifted his eyebrows and produced his PIC card. 'Find some time, sir,' he said. He smiled. 'I'd like to ask you a few questions about a company called Redbridge Holdings.'

Black's expression became even grimmer. 'I'm not surprised the police are after them,' he said. 'I hope they get what's coming to them. They're a bunch of con men.'

'How so?' Danny asked, feeling his heart begin to beat faster. It looked like he had found something! 'Are you referring to Angel Buildings?'

The man's eyes narrowed to angry slits. 'I stopped work on that place two weeks ago. I'm owed eight contractual payments.' He poked a nicotine-stained finger towards Danny. 'Do you want to know about Redbridge?' he said. 'I'll tell you something – I hope that slimy crook who runs it ends up in jail!'

Danny slipped his notebook out of his pocket. This sounded interesting...

✪

Alex sat on a wooden bench alongside the grass court. He wore aviator-style shades to keep out the dazzling midday sun. Will was being put through his paces by Johansson. The sour-faced Dane was making Will work on his weakest shots. Even with his limited knowledge of tennis, Alex could see that Will Anderson's backhand could use some attention.

The morning had been spent working out in a private gym. Alex had joined in, matching Will apparatus for apparatus. Alex loved the burn of a good work-out. He always left the gym feeling sharp and vibrant and ready for anything. Beside Alex's energetic reps, Will had seemed tired. He had worked hard, but it had all seemed like a tremendous effort. And the young tennis player was faring no better now that he was out on the grass. He hit some good shots, sending the ball rocketing back over the net, leaping high to deliver the occasional devastating passing shot that left his opponent standing. But sometimes he seemed to lack the spirit to chase a hard ball. Alex could see that Johansson was becoming frustrated.

The coach's voice sounded across the court. 'You could have reached that one! What is wrong with you?' Will looked at him with hollow eyes and sunken shoulders and walked away with his head held low.

This did not look good for Wimbledon.

'There's something wrong here,' said a deep voice over Alex's shoulder. He spun around. A grey-haired man was watching through the wire fence. Alex recognised him as one of the guys who ran the club. 'I saw Will at the French Open just a few months back. He was playing much better then; much stronger than this. Something's gone wrong recently.' The grey-haired man shook his head. 'He's lost his edge, you know.'

'He'll get it back,' Alex said.

The man looked dubious. 'I hope so,' he said. 'But I doubt it. He should be nearly at his peak now. Look at him. He's tired. He's got no life in his legs. Unless that boy does something amazing, he's going to be out of Wimbledon in the first round.'

A few minutes later, Will called for a break. He walked heavy-footed over to where Alex was sitting. He was sweating. Clearly depressed by his performance. He slumped down on to the bench next to Alex.

Johansson was staring at him from the other side of the net. It was a hard, questioning stare – as if the tall Dane was weighing up in his mind whether there was any way of motivating his young client. Will dragged his holdall between his legs and dug around in it. He brought out an opaque plastic bottle. He unscrewed the lid. He lifted the bottle to his mouth and took a swig. Johansson covered the space between the net and the bench in less time than it took Will to fill his mouth.

'What the hell do you think you're doing?' shouted the coach. He snatched the bottle out of Will's grip. Will stared at him. Startled. Alex saw the look on Johansson's face – he was angry, very angry.

'What is this?' asked the coach. He sniffed at the mouth of the bottle.

'It's just an energy drink,' Will protested. 'I've been drinking it for months. James gets it for me.'

Johansson held the bottle at arm's length. He twisted his wrist, upending the bottle. The clear liquid poured out on to the grass. 'Now, you listen to me,' he said slowly. 'I do not know what this stuff is, but from now on you eat only what I let you eat, and you drink only what I let you drink. If this is not so, then I catch the next flight out of here.' His eyebrows lowered. 'Is that understood?'

Will looked mutinous for a moment. Alex put a hand on his arm. Will subsided.

'Understood,' he said heavily.

The Dane nodded. 'Either you follow my instructions without question, or I will quit. I cannot work any other way.'

'I get the message,' Will said. 'Loud and clear.'

Lars strode away.

Will looked at Alex. 'I don't know if I can work like this,' he said in a low voice.

'Sure you can,' Alex said. 'It was never going to be easy, but you'll get used to him.'

'Maybe – but will he get used to me?' Will's eyes were anxious. 'Sometimes I think he despises me, Alex. I can't do anything right for him. Tell me one thing – if he thinks I'm a loser, why has he agreed to come here and coach me?'

Alex didn't reply. Suddenly he wasn't sure if Lars Johansson shared Will's agenda at all.

# Chapter Twelve

Wednesday.

Noon.

West London.

Danny paid the taxi driver. He straightened his jacket and looked around. He was in a dingy, run-down street in Shepherd's Bush. There were a few neglected shops. From where he was standing, Danny could smell burnt cooking oil from a grimy fish and chip shop further along the road. He searched the shop-fronts. Looking for street numbers. Getting his bearings. He wanted number 21b.

Eric Black had been a mine of angry information. The CEO of Redbridge Holdings was a man called Robert

Harris. According to Black, he ran the whole show. Black had never met him – all their dealings had been by letter or fax, with the occasional phone call. Harris had put on a good show for Eric Black, convincing him that all was well with Redbridge Holdings and that all the funding needed to start work on Angel Buildings was in place.

Everything had been fine for the first few months. Harris even paid a cash advance when the contract was signed. Then things began to slide. Bills didn't get paid. Harris made promises. The promises weren't kept. Eric Black found that he couldn't pay the men who were working in the building. Black had tried to contact Harris to sort things out. When his calls weren't returned, Black began to smell a rat. He went to Redbridge's office in Soho. A prestigious address in the centre of London. It was now an advertising agency. Robert Harris was long gone. Black had been looking for Harris ever since, but the absentee CEO of Redbridge Holdings had gone to ground.

Danny had returned to Control with all this new info. PIC had its own methods of tracking people down. An information retrieval system spread out from Control like a spider's web. Danny had quickly discovered a new address for Redbridge Holdings. Not an up-market address in Soho, but a very down-market address in Shepherd's Bush.

Danny followed the street numbers. The smell got stronger as he approached the chip shop.

A narrow alley ran alongside the shop. Above it was the number 21b. Danny walked along the passageway to a peeling door in the side wall. It opened when he pushed it. There were narrow stairs, leading up. The smell of grease followed him in. There was a pile of mail on the floor. Danny picked the letters up. They all seemed to be addressed either to Robert Harris or to Redbridge Holdings. Some were red. Unpaid bills.

Danny walked up the stairs. Light came in through a grimy window on a tiny landing halfway up the stairs. There was an unmarked door at the top, half-filled with opaque glass. Danny tried the handle. The door was locked. He paused, staring at the door. He took out his wallet and selected a suitable credit card. Then he slipped it into the doorframe, next to the lock.

It took Danny a careful, skilful minute to get the door open. It swung into a bare room that was filled with the smell of burnt fat from the chip shop downstairs. An answerphone/fax machine stood on the floor. A red light was blinking frantically – a lot of unanswered messages were stored on that machine. Page after page of white paper spewed out of the back: months of messages.

Unopened mail. Unanswered faxes. Unheard phone messages. It was obvious that this place had never been used as an office by Harris. It was just an address he had set up to throw people off his trail.

Danny pressed the playback button on the answerphone. He wandered round the empty room, listening to a series of angry messages. It sounded as though Redbridge Holdings owed a lot of money to a lot of people.

'If you were planning on a kidnapping,' he murmured to himself, 'you'd want somewhere to stash your hostages where they weren't going to be found too quickly. You wouldn't pick a half-finished apartment block in the middle of a building site unless you knew the construction crews had been called off.' He frowned. 'Interesting.'

Danny ran down the stairs, along the passageway and round the corner into the chip shop. The hot greasy air hit him like a slap in the face. A shiny-faced woman looked at him over the counter and smiled hopefully. Danny bought a portion of chips.

'Do you know who's renting the room upstairs?' he asked.

The woman shook her head. 'They come and go,' she said, wrapping the chips. 'You want to talk to the letting people. They'll know. Why? Are you interested in renting it, love?'

'D'you know where the letting agents are?' Danny asked. He avoided answering her question.

The woman told him the address. It was only two streets away. Danny took the chips and left. He binned them unopened next to a bus stop, wiping his hands fastidiously on a white handkerchief taken from his jacket pocket.

The letting agent sat at a scrupulously tidy desk behind a full-length window covered with For Sale and To Let notices. At first, the sober-faced man was reluctant to give out information about his clients. Danny's PIC ID soon persuaded him to think again.

The office over the chip shop was rented by the month. The name given was a Mr J. Smith. The rent was paid in cash, on the first Saturday of the month. Mr Smith would come into the office, hand over the money and then vanish again until the following month.

The letting agent knew nothing else about him. He had no other address. No contact phone number. Nothing. 'For all I care,' he told Danny in a surprisingly high-pitched voice, 'Mr J. Smith could beam down from

Mars once a month. As long as the rent gets paid, I don't ask questions.'

The mysterious tenant was next due at the letting agent's office in five days' time. Danny would be there. And if Mr J. Smith turned out to be Robert Harris of Redbridge Holdings, proprietor of Angel Buildings, then Danny had plenty of questions he wanted to ask him.

○

Roehampton was over. Will had made it as far as quarterfinals in this pre-Wimbledon men's tournament, and now there was only one day to go before the Wimbledon Lawn Championships themselves commenced. Will was out on court practising at Roehampton, opposite Lars Johansson. The gaunt Dane was directing all his cracking shots at Will's backhand, forcing the young player to work hard on his weakest side.

The trainer was relentless. He didn't give Will the chance to recover between rallies. He was at him all the time, ruthless and uncompromising. Balls came zinging over the net at Will. Alex guessed that most of them were travelling at well over 90 kph. There was no doubting that Johansson was a formidable opponent. But Will would be facing faster balls and much younger, much hungrier men once he was at Wimbledon.

Alex shaded his eyes against the sun. He had to admit that the new trainer's methods seemed to be paying off. Even in those few days since Johansson had been appointed, an indefinable extra edge had come into Will's game, enough to have got him to the Roehampton quarters. Alex didn't think he'd have got that far without the Dane's uncompromising coaching.

He didn't seem to be tiring quite so quickly. He was faster. His reflexes were sharper. Alex could tell that Will had noticed the change, too. He walked with a new spring in his step. He reached for difficult balls. He moved more confidently around the court.

Things were looking promising for Wimbledon.

Alex had moved into the apartment that the brothers were renting. It was in Somerset Road, overlooking the world-famous All England Lawn Tennis and Croquet Club. Alex was with Will virtually twenty-four hours a day. If anything happened – Alex would be there.

The mobile beeped in Alex's pocket.

He lifted it to his ear. 'Yes?'

'Hi, we're here.' It was Maddie's voice.

'OK.'

Alex pocketed his phone and made his way to the

front entrance to the private club. Maddie and her friend Laura Petrie were standing there. The doorman hadn't let them through. He had been given instructions not to let anyone in. The last thing Will Anderson needed in those last vital hours was to be mobbed by reporters and photographers. The media hounds were elsewhere, being fed a steady stream of stories to whet their appetite by Rufus Hawk. From what Alex could make out, the sportswear mogul had taken to the media spotlight like a duck to water.

'It's OK, Frank, they're with me,' Alex said. He winked at Maddie and grinned at Laura. She was staring into the club's reception area with wide eyes. She wore a short white dress which showed off her long dancing-fit legs, and her make-up was immaculate. Alex had to admit she looked good.

Laura had been relentless. As soon as she knew that PIC were providing 24/7 protection for Will, she was determined to meet him. After days of pleading phone calls, Maddie had given in. She had asked Alex to ask Will if it was OK. Will had said it was fine. And so Maddie had arranged to bring Laura over to Roehampton.

Alex led Maddie and Laura through the reception area to the courts.

'Oh, wow,' Laura breathed, as she caught her first sight of the young tennis player.

Johansson was pounding balls at him across the net. Sending him racing all over the court to retrieve them. But Will seemed ready for any shot the big Dane could fire at him.

Alex, Maddie and Laura watched through the fence. Not wanting to disturb the players by entering the court. Will won the shot with a spectacular, ringing forehand that left Johansson wrong-footed. The three spectators burst into applause.

Grinning, Will bowed to his audience. Alex opened the gate in the wire and beckoned to Laura and Maddie. The Dane's face was as grim as ever as he stared at them over the net. Laura walked towards Will as though in a dream. She beamed at him.

'You're my biggest fan,' she gasped.

Will raised his eyebrows and looked at Maddie.

'She means she's your biggest fan,' Maddie said. 'Will, this is Laura. Remember? The one I wanted the signed picture for?'

Will smiled, crinkling the corners of his warm brown eyes. 'Of course. Laura – how's it going?'

'It's good,' Laura replied, the colour high in her cheeks. 'It's really kind of you to let us watch you play.

I mean, you must be so nervous, with Wimbledon starting tomorrow. Not that you need to be nervous of course...' She looked helplessly at Maddie who just gazed back at her with her eyebrows raised. She was half-enjoying Laura's embarrassment – it served her right for being such a pest all week.

Will's smile broadened.

A hard voice broke into their conversation. 'We work now. We have much work still to do. No more interruptions.' Johansson glowered at Alex. 'You leave now. I insist.'

'Yes, OK, Mr Johansson,' Alex said quickly. 'We're going.'

Laura looked crestfallen that her meeting with Will was being cut short.

'I'm sorry I don't have time right now to talk to you,' Will said to her. 'Hey – why don't the two of you come along this evening? Alex can tell you all about it.'

Alex led the way out of the gate. Already, Johansson was hammering balls at Will as though he wanted to knock him right off the court.

'What's happening this evening?' Laura asked Alex.

'Rufus Hawk has arranged another press conference,' Alex said. 'He's got something new to tell everyone. Something really big.'

'What kind of big?' Maddie asked.

Alex winked at her. 'You'll just have to wait for the details like everyone else,' he said. 'But if what Will has told me is true, Rufus has done a pretty spectacular deal.' He laughed. 'It looks like Will Anderson is about to become a movie star.'

# Chapter Thirteen

Dean Street, West London.

Upstairs at the Groucho Club.

A private room.

Rows of chairs faced a long table. Reporters, sports journalists and photographers filled the chairs. At the back, BBC, ITN and Sky News camera operators fought for space. The walls were covered with the Moonrunner logo and dramatic black and white shots of Will in action on court.

Seated at the table were Will Anderson, Rufus Hawk and Lars Johansson. James stood to one side. He looked uncomfortable. Will blinked as flashing cameras ignited the air like fireworks. Rufus was grinning from ear to ear. Smug as the cat that got the cream. Alex, Laura and Maddie stood near the door.

Alex was uneasy. The crowd bothered him. They all had press passes, but how difficult would it be for someone to get their hands on a fake press pass? How difficult would it be for someone to hijack a real reporter, leave them in a heap in a back alley, and walk off with their pass?

Alex's eyes narrowed as he scanned the rows of heads. He hoped nothing bad was going to happen. He had managed to keep Will free of unpredictable crowds all week, despite Hawk getting his client on the front pages of the tabloids every day. But Hawk had insisted that Will should be at this particular shindig. And it was giving Alex a major headache.

The press conference hadn't started yet and the room was already noisy with a dozen or more overlapping conversations. Alex and Maddie had drawn slightly away from Laura, who seemed happy to lean against the wall at one side of the room, watching Will intently. Alex and Maddie spoke in low voices, their heads close together. Alex hadn't been to Centrepoint for several days – he needed to catch up.

'Danny is following a lead in Shepherd's Bush,'

Maddie told Alex. 'Everyone else is coming up empty. There's nothing on Spider.'

'That doesn't surprise me,' Alex said. 'We can rely on a professional to cover his tracks pretty thoroughly. What about Shadow?'

'Ken Lo's got five people on him, but there's been nothing so far.'

Alex gave a half smile. 'Him? Are you sure Shadow is a man? We could be dealing with a woman for all we know.'

Maddie frowned. 'Those cut-up photos didn't strike me as the sort of thing a woman would do.'

Alex looked at her. 'Why not? Remember the girlfriend Will dumped last year? She might want to get even with him. Weird things can happen when relationships go wrong.'

'Sonia Palmer?' Maddie said. 'It can't be her. We did a routine search when you told us about her. She lives in New York now.'

'That's not so far away.' Alex pursed his lips. 'I'll tell you one thing – whoever was behind that kidnapping, Hawk is milking it for all it's worth.' He nodded towards the table. 'Look at him. He's got these people eating out of his hand. Two weeks ago, they were busy sharpening the knives for Will, and now they're all over him.'

'There's no such thing as bad publicity,' Maddie said. 'Will is probably worth twice as much to Moonrunner now.'

'And Hawk is worth twice as much again,' Alex agreed. 'There can't be a person in the country who hasn't heard of Moonrunner gear by now. Look, I'm going to check things out.' He moved away from her, making his way slowly and silently round the back of the room. His trained eyes searched the crowd.

'Attention everybody, please.' Rufus Hawk's nasal voice sounded above the general conversation. 'Thank you for coming.' There was an immediate hush. 'I'd just like to kick things off by telling you that we are delighted at the progress Will is making under Lars' new training regime. We are more convinced than ever that the Wimbledon trophy is ours for the taking.'

Maddie glanced at Johansson. He sat there, expressionless as a granite statue. She couldn't make him out at all. She turned her eyes to James. He looked like a man who would rather be anywhere but here. His designer sweatshirt looked crumpled, and his forehead was beaded with sweat under the dazzling arc lights. Dark circles under his eyes suggested sleepless nights. Maddie felt a pang of sympathy. James was obviously committed to staying close to his brother, whatever the personal cost to himself.

A number of questions were fired from the floor.

'What is different about Will's new training regime?'

'How does Will feel about playing Hoffmann in the first round?'

'Can Will tell us if he is seeing anyone at the moment?'

Hawk lifted his hands. 'We'll answer all your questions later,' he said. 'First of all, I want to tell you about a very special deal that I've been negotiating over the past few days.' His voice rose unflatteringly. 'A deal with a major American film production company.' A narrow-lipped grin spread from ear to ear. 'I'm sure you'll understand why I can't name the company at this time. But I can tell you that negotiations are well advanced for Will to star in a Hollywood movie. The movie is to be called "Hostage", and Will is going to be playing a role he knows only too well – that of a brilliant young tennis star who survives a kidnap attempt, and who then goes on to single-handedly hunt down the kidnappers.' Hawk pushed back his shoulders. 'I am writing the screenplay myself.'

Maddie was impressed, despite herself. If Rufus Hawk had the connections to broker a huge deal like that, then maybe Will's career was in good hands after all — financially, at least.

Hawk's announcement was followed by a barrage of questions. Will fielded the questions with a quiet, modest charm that contrasted appealingly with Hawk's self-satisfied bluster.

Alex appeared at Maddie's side. 'Would you like me to fix you up with a bit part in the movie?' he asked with a grin. 'Will's love interest, maybe?'

Maddie laughed. 'I think you'd better talk to Laura first,' she said, nodding towards her friend.

Laura was gazing at Will. Her face looked flushed and her eyes were wide open and sparkling. Maddie thought she couldn't have looked more pleased if someone had just offered her the lead in *Swan Lake*. She's certainly got it bad for Will, Maddie said to herself. I just hope she isn't going to get hurt.

✪

The press conference was over. The reporters and photographers were gone. Laura and Maddie were sitting at the downstairs bar, keeping their eyes open for the A-list celebrities that were members of the fashionable club. Laura had one eye fixed on the door to the stairs, waiting for Will to reappear.

'What's the time?' Laura asked.

'Two minutes later than last time you asked,' Maddie said. 'Chill out, Laura! He'll be here.'

'You don't think he's gone, do you?' Laura asked. 'He wouldn't have forgotten me, would he?'

'Of course not,' Maddie said. 'Tell you what – you wait here. I'll go and see what's happening.'

She threaded her way through the crowded bar and made her way upstairs. She found the room where the press conference had been held. Rufus Hawk and Lars Johansson were still seated at the table, talking in low voices. In the room opposite, Alex had set up a makeshift PIC comm. centre with phone and laptop.

She walked further along the corridor. A door stood ajar. Maddie heard a muffled conversation. She stepped nearer. Two voices. James and Will.

'I still need you with me,' Will was saying. 'You've got to believe that.'

'Oh, really?' That was James's voice. He sounded flat and unhappy. 'You seem to be doing fine without me. Johansson's made sure of that.'

Maddie paused outside the door, not wanting to interrupt them.

'That's not true,' Will said. 'I'm feeling better in myself, that's all. I must have had some kind of virus. That's what was slowing me down. I'm over it now. It's

133

got nothing to do with Lars.' His voice was urgent. 'It was you who coached me to the top, James. I need you with me, you know that. I'd be nowhere without you.'

There was a pause. James's voice sounded thick with emotion. 'Is that true?'

'You know it is. We got this far together, didn't we? If it wasn't for Rufus and that damned contract, I'd tell Johansson to catch the next flight back home. Listen, James, there's only one person I'd rate alongside you as a coach – and that's Dad.'

Maddie bit her lip. She shouldn't be listening to this, but she was afraid that the brothers might hear her if she tried to creep away.

'Do you ever think about those times?' James asked quietly.

'Yes.'

'Before the accident?'

'I think about it a lot.' Will's voice was as subdued as his brother's. 'Do you?'

'Yes. Remember the old house in Chislehurst? Remember playing doubles in the garden with Mum and Dad?'

Will laughed softly. 'Me and Dad versus you and Mum. I remember it like it was yesterday.'

'And Mrs Greer as umpire,' James laughed.

'That's right. She was always bringing us that sickly home-made lemonade. She said it would give us energy!'

Maddie smiled. She remembered the name from the Internet site: Mrs Greer, the Andersons' next-door neighbour. The woman who took James and Will to hospital after the fall from the tree. They sounded like they still had a lot of affection for her.

James laughed from beyond the door. 'And she didn't have a clue about the rules of tennis,' he said. 'And she kept calling the rackets "bats".'

'She moved, didn't she?' Will said. 'Not long after Mum and Dad... you know...'

'Yes,' James said. 'I don't know where to, though.'

'Pity,' Will said. 'It would have been great if we could have invited her along to Wimbledon. She'd have liked that.'

Maddie's ears pricked up. An idea came to her — something that would mean a lot to the brothers. She would find Mrs Greer for them. She could use PIC to find her. Then, she'd invite her to Wimbledon. But she wouldn't tell James and Will yet. It would be a surprise for them. The decision made, Maddie tapped on the door.

James opened it wider. Will was standing just behind him.

'Sorry to disturb you, guys,' she said, brightly. 'But there's someone down in the bar who is absolutely dying to talk to you, Will.'

'Laura! Of course,' Will said. 'I'm so sorry – I forgot all about her.' He grabbed his jacket from the back of a chair. 'I'll go down right now.'

'You'll find her in the main bar,' Maddie said.

'I'll leave you to it,' James said. He picked up a newspaper from a low table in the centre of the room and sat down in an armchair by the window.

Will pulled his jacket on and walked quickly down the corridor. A door opened and Alex appeared.

'Where's Will going?' he asked.

Maddie smiled at him. 'He's off to make Laura's day,' she said.

'He's not meant to wander about on his own,' Alex said. 'I'd better go after him.'

Maddie said goodbye to James, and followed Alex along the corridor.

'Don't be too obvious,' Maddie said. 'Let Laura have him all to herself for a few minutes. She's totally crazy about him.'

Alex looked sharply at her. 'Why do you say that?'

Maddie shrugged. 'She thinks he's great, that's all I meant.' She frowned. 'Why?'

'Shadow is probably crazy,' Alex said slowly.

Maddie stared at him in disbelief. 'You think *Laura* could be Shadow?' she gasped. 'That's ridiculous. I've known her all my life!'

Alex shrugged. 'No,' he said. 'I don't think Laura is Shadow. But it could be someone like her – some over-obsessed fan who's flipped their lid and gone psycho.' He looked at Maddie. 'And it's like I said before – if you want my opinion, Shadow is just as likely to be a woman as a man.'

# Chapter Fourteen

Friday evening at the Coopers' apartment.

Maddie was lying on the couch. Gran was sitting at the window, leafing through a glossy magazine. The TV was on. It was the fifth day of Wimbledon. Maddie was watching the highlights of Will Anderson's match against a favoured Spaniard in the third round. Laura was on the phone.

'Did you see the way he beat Joel Sherwood?' Laura said. 'Three straight sets. He blew him off the court. And Sherwood is ranked 37th in the world. Will is only 61st right now, but he deserves to be much higher. He was 32nd last year, but he slipped down the ranks when he bombed out at the Australian

Open in January. Did you see him? Wasn't he brilliant?'

'I only saw a few games on the news,' Maddie said. She winced as Will dived for a tricky ball and missed. One set down. The replay jumped ahead to the third game. Will broke the Spaniard's serve. Maddie had to hold the phone away from her ear to avoid being deafened by Laura's cheering.

'Chill out!' Maddie shouted down the phone. 'I thought you said you'd already watched this match this afternoon.'

'I did, but it's still brilliant. Will's in command all the way now. He ends up beating the other guy three sets to one. The Spaniard doesn't win a single game in the last set. It's killer!'

Maddie rolled her eyes. 'Way to ruin the match for me, Laura!' she said.

'Oh. Sorry. I thought you knew.'

'I didn't.'

'Have you had any luck finding Will's old neighbour?' Laura changed the subject. Maddie told her about her plan to track Mrs Greer down.

'I think so,' Maddie said. 'I've got an address in Brighton. I haven't had much time. We've been pretty busy at work. First chance I get, I'm going to call her and invite her up to Wimbledon.'

They talked for a few minutes more. After Laura had gone, Maddie turned the TV off, mid-match. Her gran raised questioning eyebrows. Maddie leaned over the back of the couch. 'She told me the final score!' she explained. 'There's no point watching it if I know what's going to happen.'

'He's doing well, isn't he?' Gran said, closing the magazine and placing it on a glass-topped table. 'He sailed through the first couple of rounds. Let's hope he can keep it up. And let's hope he can put all that unpleasantness with the kidnapping behind him.'

'He's coping with it really well,' Maddie said. 'Alex thinks that Shadow is a crazy fan. The general feeling at Control is that Shadow never really intended to involve the hit man at all.' She shook her head. 'They think Shadow just wanted to do something that would make the headlines, which is why Will and Alex were left to escape so easily after the kidnapping. They reckon he'll back off now. I'm not so sure.'

Gran looked thoughtful. 'So all those threats were just a publicity stunt? That seems a rather extreme way to generate attention. If I were being sent death threats, I would be more likely to stay in hiding, I must say, not spend time with the press.'

Her gran had a point, Maddie realised. Will's short-lived abduction seemed harmless compared with the viciousness of the mind which had tried to hire a killer. Maddie hadn't forgotten those pictures of Will. The ones that had plastered the walls of that nasty little room. The ones with the eyes missing. Cut out. Torn out. Burned out. It was a difficult image to forget. It was even more difficult to imagine the mind of the person who would do such a thing. If Maddie's intuition was right, it was not a mind that would be satisfied with a failed kidnap attempt. Something told her that Will would be needing their help before very long.

It wasn't over. It wasn't over by a long way.

✪

Saturday.

Danny was sitting at a desk in the back of the letting agent's office in Shepherd's Bush. He had been there for four hours already. There was nothing much going on – just three customers all day. The gloomy guy on the front desk had dealt with them. Danny had tried to strike up a conversation, but the guy was too gloomy to talk.

Smith was due any time. Danny poured strong black coffee from a flask. It kept him alert. All he could do was sit quietly, drink the rapidly cooling coffee and eat limp day-old sandwiches he had bought from the newsagent across the road. Waiting. And thinking.

He'd pick up J. Smith. Smith would lead him to Harris. Harris would tell them something that would give them a lead on Shadow. Assuming that Shadow was responsible for the kidnapping, and therefore had some connection with Angel Buildings. That was the plan. When PIC had finished with Harris, he'd be handed over to the Fraud Squad, where a whole bunch of angry creditors would be waiting to talk to him.

Shadow had to have known that work had been suspended on Angel Buildings. How could he know that? Either there was a link to the contractors, or there was a link to Redbridge Holdings.

Another PIC officer was already digging for the possible HCGM Construction link. Danny was here to join the dots from Smith to Shadow. If the guy ever turned up.

Danny drank some more coffee. He shifted in the cheap office chair, trying to make himself more comfortable. Time passed. Between the thin cardboard For Sale and To Let signs that covered the windows, Danny saw a dark-blue BMW cruise slowly along the street. It swooped into the kerb outside the letting agent's office and came to a stop.

'That's him,' said the letting agent. He sounded

bored, unimpressed at the prospect of police action being carried out in his office.

'OK,' Danny said. 'Play it cool. Act natural. I'll do the rest.'

The driver's door opened. A man got out. Danny's eyes widened. 'You're kidding me?' he murmured. He knew the guy. Now *this*, he hadn't been expecting. No way. The man closed the car door. He came in through the glass door of the letting agent's office. The door closed behind him.

Danny smiled. The man didn't even notice him sitting back there. He took a large brown wallet from his inside jacket pocket.

Danny stood up. His chair scraped on the plastic-tiled floor. The man glanced briefly at him. The letting agent looked around too, his eyebrows raised. The man started counting out banknotes from the bulging wallet. He spotted that he had lost the agent's attention. He looked at Danny. His eyes narrowed, as if he was trying to remember where he had seen Danny's face before.

Danny smiled. 'Hi, there,' he said calmly. 'We met at Will Anderson's launch party.' Danny took out his PIC ID card. 'Remember?'

The man's face drained of colour. He didn't speak.

'I think we need to have a chat – back at my office.' Danny's smile widened. 'If that's OK with you, Mr Hawk.'

✪

Maddie spent Saturday afternoon watching the tennis on TV. Every now and then she tried the phone number she had tracked down for Mrs Greer. A Brighton number. The phone seemed to be permanently engaged. Finally, she got suspicious. She phoned directory enquiries. There was a fault with the line. Maddie felt very disappointed. She still had the address, so there was always the option of writing to Mrs Greer – but that would take too long. Besides, Maddie had a better idea.

She went through into her bedroom. She booted up her PC and logged on to the Internet. It only took her ten minutes to book herself a return train ticket to Brighton for the following day. She was going to take a train down to the coast, and – with any luck – she was going to meet Mrs Greer in person.

✪

It was the first Sunday of the Wimbledon Championships. A rest day from the tournament. Will and James were in their apartment in Somerset Road. Alex was out. He had gone back to his own place for a few hours to sort out some fresh clothes and to check that everything was OK over there.

Will planned on spending a few hours in the practice courts later on in the day, but right now he was out on the balcony enjoying breakfast in the early-morning sunshine. Relaxing. Feeling great. Reading the Sunday papers. Soaking up all the praise that was being heaped on him. Finding it exhilarating and odd at the same time.

James came out with a thick white envelope in his hand. It had Will's name on it – but no address. 'It must have been delivered by hand,' James said, dropping it on his brother's plate. He smiled. He looked more relaxed than he had done for days. 'More fan mail.'

An ordinary white envelope with Will's name written on it in black capital letters.

Will picked the envelope up and opened it. He looked into the envelope and frowned. He turned the envelope upside down and shook it.

James jumped back. A flattened tarantula had dropped on to the table, black, hairy and very dead. Beside it lay a small black card, about twice the size of a credit card. It was stained with a yellowish fluid which had leaked out of the dead spider. The writing on the card was in silver. Block capitals. Painstakingly, obsessively neat.

KEEP YOUR EYES OPEN ANDERSON, THERE'S A SPIDER IN THE SHADOWS.

# Chapter Fifteen

A room. Small and square with white walls. No windows. One plain table. Seated to one side of the table were Danny and Jack Cooper. Facing them was Rufus Hawk. The table also bore the remains of a curling sandwich on a plate. Three white plastic coffee cups. And a black digital recording device. A red light indicated that it was on.

Danny looked at Hawk. He was as miserable and deflated as a burst water wing. He looked in shock, as if he couldn't believe that all his schemes had fallen apart. Rufus Hawk was spilling his guts.

Smith – the guy who rented the office in Shepherd's Bush – was Rufus Hawk. But more importantly, Rufus

Hawk was also Robert Harris – CEO of Redbridge Holdings.

'The problems started when I set up the Internet site for Moonrunner,' Hawk told them. 'It cost far more than I'd expected. I invested every penny I had to get the site up and running. But it didn't pay its way. I had to borrow money from my other businesses to bail it out.' His shoulders slumped. 'It ended up swallowing everything. I'm completely broke.'

'So, you signed Will Anderson up with the promise that you would sponsor his career,' Danny said, 'knowing all along that you couldn't even afford to sponsor him to go buy a tube of toothpaste, is that right?'

A sick gleam of light ignited behind Hawk's eyes. 'He was going to save me,' he said hoarsely. 'That was the whole idea. Will would generate money. I would be able to loan him out to other people. They'd pay me. Big money. Top tennis stars are worth a fortune. Once I was back on my feet, I'd have been able to make good on my promises to him.' He spread his hands. His voice rose. He almost sounded convinced again. 'Do you see? Everything would have been fine.'

'You actually linked up with Will Anderson back in January,' Jack Cooper said.

'That's right,' Hawk said. 'Just before the Australian Open. He was expected to get to the final.' His face became desperate. 'Everyone was saying that he'd get to the final.'

'But he bombed out in round one,' Danny said. 'And all of a sudden, he wasn't such a hot property any more.'

'I'd planned on breaking the news about the sponsorship deal after he won,' Hawk said. 'But he didn't win. We talked it over, and we decided it would be better to leave the official announcement until just before Wimbledon. You know – make a big splash of it. And that way, it would give him plenty of time to get back into form.'

'Except that his form didn't improve,' Jack Cooper said. 'So you came up with your big idea.'

Hawk looked sick. 'It was just a publicity stunt,' he croaked. 'Will was never going to be hurt. I made sure of that.' He ran his tongue over his lips. 'I set it up with four guys from the building site – I had seen them working there. They looked tough enough to make it seem real, but I told them right from the start that it was just a stunt – no one was going to get hurt.' His eyes were desperate. 'You have to believe that – I never intended any harm to come to anyone. I just thought it would give Will an extra publicity boost – to get people interested in him again. To get him in the news.' He rubbed his hands through his hair, which was damp with sweat. 'There is no movie deal, either,' he went on quietly. 'The whole thing was fake.' He stared at the two police officers, looking suddenly thoughtful. 'Is there some way you can let me off the hook? I'll make it worth your while.' He sounded brisk and businesslike again.

Danny suppressed a smile. Rufus Hawk was trying to bargain with them. Some chance! Jack Cooper looked at the crestfallen man for a few penetrating moments.

'Tell us about Shadow,' he said.

Hawk looked taken aback. 'Shadow? I don't know anything about Shadow,' he said. 'He's just some crazy man, isn't he? That's what I was told.'

'Maybe not so crazy,' Cooper said. 'We think Shadow could be the same man who rang you, threatening Will Anderson in the run-up to the kidnapping.'

'No, no, no,' Hawk said vehemently. 'I set that up. I've told you, it was just a stupid publicity stunt. I don't know anything about these other things.' His eyes flickered from Danny to Cooper. 'You're trying to fit me up!' he accused them. 'I'm not saying another thing until I get a lawyer.'

'Don't worry, Mr Hawk,' Cooper growled. 'You'll get your lawyer.' He looked at his watch. 'Interview terminated at eleven forty-three, pending the arrival of Rufus Hawk's lawyer.' He pressed the button on the recorder and the red light went out. Jack Cooper manoeuvred his wheelchair away from the table. He pushed himself towards the door.

'Danny?' he said over his shoulder. 'A word.'

They closed the door of the interview room. Cooper looked up at Danny.

'Well?' he asked. 'What do we think?'

Danny shook his head. 'I believe him,' he said. 'He's a slime ball and an idiot and a crook – but I don't think he's a psycho.'

Cooper stared grimly ahead. 'Unfortunately, I agree with you,' he said. 'Which leaves us with a problem.'

Danny nodded. 'Shadow's still out there.'

'And Will Anderson is still in danger.' Cooper began to wheel himself along the hallway. Danny followed. 'You'd better get on to Alex – get him up to speed. We've still got work to do.'

✪

'I can't believe it.' Will was sitting on the balcony of the rented house in Somerset Road. James was with him. So was Alex. Alex had just told the brothers about the

151

arrest of Rufus Hawk. Will's face was ashen. Stunned. James's face showed only anger.

'You know what this means, don't you?' he said to Will. His voice was strained. 'There's no money. If Hawk is penniless, we can't pay for anything. This apartment. The equipment. It was all organised by Hawk – and he can't cover the bills.'

'We can deal with that,' Will said. 'We've got enough money to pay our way.'

'We don't have enough to pay Johansson's wages,' James said.

Will plucked restlessly at the white linen tablecloth. 'No,' he agreed. 'We don't have that kind of money.' He looked into James's face. 'You and me again, huh?' He smiled. 'So, it's not all bad news.' He ran a hand through his hair. 'The Anderson boys are back in action.' He looked at Alex. 'Does Lars know about this yet?'

Alex shook his head.

'I'll tell him,' said James. He sounded calmer now, more in control. 'That'll be a nasty shock for him. My guess is, he'll be on the next flight back to Denmark.'

Alex watched Will carefully. 'Has something else happened?' he asked him. 'You guys seem really strung up this morning.'

Will took a long, deep breath. 'I'll be fine,' he said.

His eyes became steely. 'I'm not going to let all this get to me.' He lifted an arm and cut his hand through the air like the prow of the ship cleaving water. 'Eyes on the prize. Total focus. The Championship is all that matters. Forget everything else.' He put his hand firmly on the table. 'Forget the threats. Forget everything.'

Alex looked at James. 'What threats?'

The brothers looked uneasily at one another.

'There's been some weird stuff,' James said at last. 'Warnings, I suppose.'

Alex frowned. 'You should have told me.'

'I'm not being put off my game,' Will said. 'Shadow might be out of his mind, but he's not going to drive me crazy. And he's not going to wreck my chance of winning this tournament.'

Alex shook his head. He gazed steadily at James. These brothers were close, but they weren't invincible, and they would have to let him help if Will's safety was to be guaranteed. 'I have to know exactly what's been going on,' he said. 'And from now on, you tell me everything, OK? *Everything*.'

✪

Maddie emerged from Brighton train station. The street fell away in a long curve towards the sea front. All the shops were open and there were plenty of people about. The curve of the street hid the sea, but the air had a faint, salty tang. Gulls drifted in the air and screamed to one another.

Maddie had printed out a local street map. She had highlighted the route to Mrs Greer's road. She took a left turn. She hoped Mrs Greer still lived there. It was a long way to come for nothing. She found herself in Trafalgar Street. She needed to cross over the Grand Parade and make her way to Southover Street. She caught a glimpse of the shining domes of the Pavilion.

Maddie walked along Southover Street, checking the names of the side streets. She found the one she wanted. The houses were tall and elegant, with large windows which gave glimpses of airy, high-ceilinged rooms inside.

She came to number 43. She walked up the stone steps and rang the doorbell. There was no response. Maddie frowned. If her journey was going to end in disappointment, she was glad she hadn't told the brothers of her plan.

She turned to make her way back down to street level when she heard a noise. She turned back to the door. Several seconds passed before the door opened. A gaunt face peered at her through the dark crack. The eyes were pale and watery. Thin white hair was scraped back and held with a tortoiseshell comb.

'Hello,' Maddie said, smiling at the old woman. 'My name is Maddie Cooper. I'm looking for Mrs Marion Greer.'

'That's me.' The voice sounded weak but surprised. Maddie held out her PIC ID and waited while Mrs Greer studied it.

The door opened slightly wider. Maddie saw the aluminium bars of a Zimmer frame. The woman was in dressing gown and slippers.

'I'm sorry,' Maddie said. 'Did I get you out of bed?'

'That's all right, dear.' The old lady smiled. 'It's high time I was up anyway. What can I do for you?'

Maddie couldn't think of what to say. It looked like the sick old lady was housebound. She was certainly in no state to take a trip up to Wimbledon. It seemed to Maddie that her journey to Brighton had been a waste of time after all.

## Chapter Sixteen

'I've always kept an eye on Will's career – on the TV and in the newspapers,' Mrs Greer said. She held a kettle under the kitchen tap and turned it on. 'He's been a bit off form recently. I was expecting him to win the Australian Open, you know. Still, you can't come top every time. Someone has to lose.' She turned off the tap and put the kettle on the side, pressing the switch.

'He's doing really well at Wimbledon,' Maddie said. 'Have you been watching?'

Mrs Greer nodded. 'He's a good boy,' she said. 'They're both lovely. I never had children of my own, so those boys were very special to me. They used to call me Auntie G.' Her eyes focused on a spot beyond

Maddie. 'You know, dear, when they were boys, it was difficult to say who was the better tennis player. James had four years on Will, of course, so he was bigger and stronger. But I think Will was the most gifted – even then, even when he was just little.' She sighed. 'It was such a shame about James, though.'

'A shame?' echoed Maddie.

'The accident,' Mrs Greer said. 'Don't you know about the accident?'

'Oh, yes – of course,' Maddie said. 'They fell out of a tree.'

'That's right, the poor mites.' Mrs Greer's eyes became sad. 'The first I knew about it was the boys shouting. Shouting at one another. Then there was a cracking noise. Wood breaking, you know. It was the branch. It must have been rotten, because it broke like a twig. They fell right over the fence into my rose bush.' She shook her head, her eyes screwed up. 'Poor Will was knocked out on a paving stone, and James was on the ground, screaming in pain and holding his eye. I put them in my car and took them straight to hospital. Their parents were out for the day, you see. At first I thought Will was worse off, but he woke up after a few minutes, and all he had was a splitting headache. It was James who was really badly hurt. He's blind in one eye, you know. He never played tournament tennis again. You can't judge the ball with only one eye.'

'I read about it,' Maddie said. 'It must have been bad.'

Mrs Greer nodded. 'I have something I can show you,' she said. 'Just you wait there. I won't be a minute.'

She shuffled across the cracked lino, supporting herself on her Zimmer.

'Can I help?' Maddie offered, standing up.

'No, no. I must exercise as much as I can.' She smiled. 'Doctor's orders.'

While Mrs Greer was gone, Maddie poured hot water into the teapot and found two cups on the draining board.

Mrs Greer returned with a garishly patterned plastic photo album under her arm. She put the album on the table. She turned over the heavy, stiff leaves. Black-and-white and colour photos. She opened the album to a page with a newspaper clipping in it. The headline was NEIGHBOUR'S MERCY DASH.

A black-and-white newspaper photograph showed a middle-aged Mrs Greer standing between two boys – the Anderson brothers, much younger, but still clearly recognisable. Will, with his round, baby-face, and James, his face already longer and more angular, a white bandage angled across his head, covering his damaged eye. They were standing under a tree.

Mrs Greer tapped the picture with a thin, crooked finger. 'This got into the local paper. The boys were well known locally. They were the big stars of the local tennis club – even at that age.'

Maddie leaned forward to look at the photograph.

'One thing has puzzled me all these years,' Mrs Greer went on thoughtfully.

'What's that?' Maddie prompted gently.

Mrs Greer looked up at her, as if only just realising she'd been speaking aloud. 'Oh, it's nothing, really; just one of those little things. Will was a silly boy to have gone up that tree on his own. He never had a good head for heights. It was James who liked climbing – not Will.' She shrugged. 'I expect Will was just trying to be like his brother.' She shook her head. 'The silly boy.'

○

Monday.

The Millennium Building at the Wimbledon All England Lawn Tennis & Croquet Club.

Alex, Will, James and Lars Johansson were in the changing room. Will was getting ready for his next match. He had fought through to the fourth round. This would be a hard one. Owen Knight was a powerful

American with plenty of Grand Slam appearances under his belt. His speciality was a blistering ace. In his last match, he had blown his opponent off court.

'Do not be intimidated,' Johansson was saying to Will. 'You can beat this man. He is fast and strong – but he thinks like a machine. He is not good at improvising. He has not much brain. You have plenty. Keep him guessing. Don't let him get into a rhythm. You can beat him if you do this. But you must concentrate.'

Will nodded as he tied his shoes.

Alex kept well out of the way, watching the three men. Like Will and James, he was amazed that Lars Johansson was there at all. They had all expected the sour-faced Dane to walk out the moment he was told the truth about Rufus Hawk. But to their surprise, Lars had stayed.

'It's not your fault that your sponsor is a crook,' he had said to Will. 'I will not abandon a client in the middle of a tournament.' His eyes had flashed. 'You will pay me out of your winnings, no?' A very rare joke from the grim coach.

James had shown no ill-feeling at Johansson's presence, but Alex felt sure that he must have been disappointed to be denied the chance to step back into his role as coach.

Will picked up his holdall. He was ready. The four of them made their way to court 19.

A man approached them on their way to court. He was carrying in his arms a long white box. Alex recognised him. He was one of the Honorary Stewards.

'This came for you, Mr Anderson,' he said.

Startled by the interruption to his pre-match routine, Will put down his holdall and took the box. The way he held it made it clear to Alex that whatever was in it did not weigh very much.

Will took the lid off the box. Inside, wrapped in white tissue paper blotted with dark red stains, were a dozen dead roses. Their wilted petals were black and shrivelled. Their leaves were withered. A dreadful stench wafted from the box, thick and meaty.

Will stood staring into the box. He seemed stunned. His face was white.

Alex stepped forwards and snatched the box out of his arms. 'Go and play your match,' he said.

'That smell...' James began, putting his hand over his mouth. He looked as if he wanted to vomit.

Alex looked down at the box, trying hard not to gag. An oozing brownish lump nestled beside the brittle stalks. 'It's just a piece of meat,' he said roughly. 'It's nothing.' He pushed the lid back on to the box.

Will looked helplessly round at them. He seemed unable to move. Johansson stared into Will's eyes, as if trying to assess the damage that had been done.

'Forget this,' the coach said. 'Focus on the match. Concentrate. Mr Cox will deal with this. That is why he is here.'

Alex nodded. James reached out with one hand, as if he wanted to comfort Will, then let it fall limply back to his side. Will picked up his holdall and began to walk away. With a despairing look at Alex, James followed him.

Johansson glared at Alex. 'You are here to stop this,' he barked. 'You are of no use!' He turned and strode after the two brothers.

Taking a deep breath of clean air, Alex opened the box again. He lifted the folds of stained tissue paper and drew out a small black card. It was printed with a shadowy black-and-white image of an open, staring eye. Words were scrawled on top of the image in brownish-red ink.

*I have my eye on you, Anderson. See you soon.*

○

Monday evening.

Maddie got home from work in time to watch the highlights of the day's play on TV. The news was good. Will Anderson had battled through against the 11th seed Owen Knight in a marathon five-setter.

Lapses in concentration had cost Will the second and fourth sets, but he had won the fifth, six games to love, finally knocking the spirit out of Owen Knight with a match-winning ace that scorched the air and nearly poleaxed a linesman.

In the post-match interview, Will looked tired but thrilled. He was asked how the troubles with Rufus Hawk had affected him. Hawk's arrest and confession were big news. Now, reporters were digging into Hawk's business practices – finding more dirt all the time. It was a media sensation.

Will shrugged the question off. 'It's not relevant to the way I'm thinking right now,' he said. 'My focus is entirely on my next match. I can't let Rufus Hawk's behaviour affect me. Besides, I have a very supportive team. My brother is with me, and Lars Johansson has agreed to stay at least until the end of the tournament.'

'Can you see yourself holding the Challenge Cup?' the BBC presenter asked.

Will smiled. 'I certainly hope so,' he said.

The interview finished with a shot of Will jogging towards the changing rooms. The presenter turned to the camera with a practised smile and began to summarise the day's other matches.

Maddie turned the TV off and fiddled absent-mindedly with the fringe on a cushion. She was thinking about her meeting with Mrs Greer. The old lady had asked her not to tell James and Will that she was unwell.

'Tell them after Wimbledon,' she had said. 'I wouldn't want them worrying about me at a time like this. I'll still be here when the tournament is over. They can come and visit me, if they'd like to. I'd enjoy that.'

Maddie frowned. Mrs Greer had said that Will wasn't good with heights. Then why had he climbed up the tree? It was odd. And there was something else. Something about that newspaper photograph. Something that didn't quite add up.

Maddie reached over to the coffee table and picked up the faded newspaper article. Mrs Greer had been quite happy for Maddie to borrow it for a while, with a promise of its safe return. Maddie studied the photo. Will on Mrs Greer's left, his baby-face and mop of light-brown hair, not quite reaching to the level of her shoulder. Eleven-year-old James to her right, a good half a head higher than his brother. His face crossed by that white bandage. The three of them standing in front of the tall old tree with its long, smooth trunk and broad spread of leaf-laden branches.

What was wrong with the picture? Maddie frowned. Maybe it was nothing.

The phone rang. She laughed softly to herself. She could guess who it was. She picked up. 'Hello, Laura,' she said. 'Yes, I saw it. Yes, he was great. And yes, I do realise that he's in the quarterfinals now.'

✪

```
SPIDER: I wasn't expecting to hear from you
        again.
SHADOW: My plans didn't work out.
SPIDER: Is the job still on?
```

The briefest of pauses, then:

```
SHADOW: Yes.
SPIDER: Elimination?
```

A longer pause.

```
SHADOW: Yes.
SPIDER: I will need full details.
SHADOW: I want the target eliminated at a
        precise time and in a particular way.
        Can you do that?
SPIDER: Yes.
```

```
SHADOW: I can't give you all the details yet.
SPIDER: Understood. Contact me again 6 hours
        before the elimination is to take
        place. I will give you a mobile-phone
        number. Use it only once — to confirm
        or abort the job. We will need to
        agree code words. If the job is
        terminated, I will still require
        payment in full. Is that understood?
SHADOW: Yes. I understand.
```

The connection was cut.

Shadow leaned back. Shaking uncontrollably. Sweating. Heart pounding.

Revenge was coming.

# Chapter Seventeen

Friday evening.

The men's semifinals; Will Anderson versus Yuri Ulyanov.

Maddie was glued to the match replay.

It was frustrating to watch. Will didn't make things easy for his supporters. Just when he seemed to have the game in the bag, he'd make some unforced errors, or he'd lose concentration, and the whole flow of the match would turn against him. Two sets up, he lost the next two sets without once breaking his opponent's serve. Then he rallied, winning the final set six-four.

Then there were the interviews.

'Will Anderson – that was quite a fight – but you won through in the end.'

Will smiled engagingly. 'Yes.' There was pleasure and relief in his voice. 'Yuri is a good player. Every game is a challenge at this level, but I knew he would be hard work.'

Looking at Will, strained and exhilarated after his victory, it was difficult for Maddie to believe in the death threat that was looming over him. But it was real enough. It had not gone away. Alex had told her about the dead roses and the rotten meat. But sending the roses had been Shadow's last act so far – nothing had happened all week.

Maddie didn't find that comforting – she found it ominous.

The telephone rang. Laura, of course. She was making plans for the final.

'I'm having some of the guys over to watch it at my place,' Laura said. 'Susanna and Jules and Jacqueline, hopefully. Will you be able to come, Maddie?'

'I can't,' Maddie said. 'I've got to work.'

'You've got to work?' Laura almost yelled. 'On the day of the Wimbledon men's final? Is your dad some kind of sadist or what?'

'That's the way it goes,' Maddie said. 'Sorry. You guys have a good time.'

She didn't tell Laura what work she was being asked

to do. Maddie and Danny and Alex would all be at Centre Court for the final. Along with a squad of PIC officers, their job would be to keep their eyes open for anything unusual in the crowd. Jack Cooper's biggest fear was that Shadow would make his move during the final. He intended to draft every available officer into the Wimbledon area.

Nothing was going to happen to Will Anderson in front of a global TV audience, Jack Cooper was determined about that.

○

Over the two-week period of the Championship, almost nine hundred people are employed for security and crowd control at Wimbledon. Honorary Stewards, security guards, volunteers from the armed forces and officers of the London Fire Brigade – they all play their part. This year there were also going be fifteen officers from PIC. In the North Hall of the Centre Court building, there is an office for the Metropolitan Police. Chief Superintendent Jack Cooper commandeered the well-equipped room for PIC Control.

Wimbledon-fever reached its height on the day of the men's final. The newspapers featured little else. An electrifying seventeen-year-old Brit had made it to the final. Will Anderson was everyone's hero. Anyone switching on a television or radio, picking up a newspaper or listening to a conversation in the shops or streets, would be forgiven for thinking the entire country had gone tennis-mad.

Rufus Hawk would have been ecstatic about it. If not for the fact that Hawk was on remand in Brixton Prison and didn't have access to a television set on Sunday afternoon. He sat through the final with his head in his hands, wondering where he had gone wrong.

Centre Court was packed. The overspill crowded on to the grass of the Aorangi Picnic Terraces to the west of No. 1 Court, preparing to watch the match on a giant TV screen. The atmosphere was festive and excited and sparking with the anticipation of a great match.

The sky was overcast, and the air felt sticky and humid. It was going to be sweltering on Centre Court. Maddie and Danny sat in the front row, directly behind the umpire's tower. Alex was on the far side of the court, in a block of seats alongside the scoreboard reserved for the players' families and teams. Sitting with him were Lars Johansson and Will's aunt and uncle. James's seat was still empty.

The linesmen stood at each end of the court in their immaculate purple and green uniforms. The umpire came out to a polite ripple of applause and climbed the steps to her chair.

TV cameras panned the court, their lenses winking as they caught the pale sun. Danny was monitoring the TV coverage live on his laptop.

'Can you see us?' Maddie asked, leaning over his shoulder. She knew they were here for a serious purpose, but it was hard not to get caught up in the celebratory mood of the crowd.

The screen showed a dizzying aerial view of the court from the BBC cherry-picker crane. Someone in the TV studio was reeling off statistics about record attendances and sales of strawberries. The shot changed to the green doors behind the scoreboard.

'Here we go,' said Danny. Maddie looked down at the laptop. Someone was holding one of the doors open.

A white-clad figure emerged. The crowd erupted.

Will Anderson and Craig Tanner walked on to Centre Court with their holdalls slung over their shoulders. Australian Tanner was the number two seed. He'd thrashed the number one in the semifinals. Will was unseeded. This was the first time the two men had clashed, but with Will's current blazing form, the bookies were divided about the outcome of the match.

Maddie heard a tinny voice above the applause. It was Alex, speaking to her via an earpiece plugged into her mobile phone.

'Maddie? Have you seen James?'

'No,' she replied, dropping her head to speak into the earpiece's built-in mike. 'He should be with you.'

'He isn't,' Alex said.

'What's up?' Danny asked, looking up from the laptop.

'James is missing,' Maddie told him.

'Maybe he was in the changing room with Will,' Danny suggested.

Maddie relayed this to Alex. 'I'll check it out,' Alex said. 'Tara is down there – she'll know.'

Alex broke contact with Maddie.

The two players began to warm up, hitting easy balls across the net to one another. Ball boys and girls scuttled around like green and purple liveried beetles. Tension mounted.

The umpire's voice rang out. 'Two minutes, please, gentlemen.'

Will pulled his sweatshirt over his head and draped it over the back of his chair. He saw Maddie and Danny and gave them a wave. He seemed relaxed and full of energy.

The Australian took his position at one end of the court and waited. Will rotated his shoulders, picked up his racket, and walked steadily to his place.

The crowd became quiet.

Will was first to serve. He bounced the ball. Arched his back. With his racket poised he threw the ball high. It spun for a moment. His arm swung. The head of his racket hit the ball squarely. The ball zipped across the net.

The Championship final had begun.

○

A buzz of different voices sounded in Danny's ear. He had linked his laptop into the PIC security network. He rolled the mouse-ball, changing from channel to channel. He listened to his colleagues one by one.

Nothing to report.

'Good,' Danny murmured to himself. 'Nothing to report is good.'

There was a roar of applause. He looked up. The umpire's voice rang out.

'Game and first set, Anderson.'

Maddie scanned the crowds with her miniature binoculars. She focused on a man sitting opposite her with swept-back brown hair and deep-set eyes. Will's uncle. His wife sat next to him, a petite dark-haired woman wearing a pale-yellow shirt. The seat next to them was vacant. Then came Lars Johannson, his stony face as expressionless as ever. He wasn't even applauding – just watching Will with an intensity that reminded Maddie of a bird of prey.

The other seats in the block were filled with Craig Tanner's entourage. Supermodel girlfriend, aloof in designer shades. Mother and father, flown in from Australia and looking flushed and proud.

She scanned back to the empty seat. Maddie pressed a preset button on her mobile and opened a channel to Alex.

'Any sign of James?' she asked.

'I don't think so. I spoke to Tara. She hasn't seen him. We've got someone at their apartment – he's not there either.'

'Do you think something's happened to him?' Maddie asked. Her stomach clenched with fear. Might Shadow have fooled them all? While their attention was fixed on Will, Shadow could have taken James instead. If someone wanted to hurt Will, they could guarantee he would be devastated if anything happened to his brother.

'I spoke to the boss,' Alex said. 'He's alerted everyone, but he says we should stick to our posts. If

James has been abducted, it might be a deliberate move to draw us away from Will.'

The end of the first set. After a hard-won victory, Will was sitting in his chair with his back to Danny and Alex. There was a towel draped around his shoulders. He was swigging from a bottle of fruit squash. It was hot out there. The stadium was like an oven.

The angle of Will's head changed. Danny guessed he was looking up to where James should have been sitting. Will turned in his seat, looking at Maddie and Danny. His eyes were questioning. He had seen that James was still not there.

'Uh-oh,' Danny muttered to himself. 'He won't like that.'

Maddie made a discreet gesture to Will, trying to indicate that people were looking for James. She mouthed, 'Don't worry,' to him. She didn't know if it would do any good.

'Time, please,' came the umpire's voice.

The two players got up.

Maddie felt her nails dig into her palms. How would Will cope with his brother's absence? Would it affect his game?

❁

The mood of the crowd had changed. Too often during the second set, there was the silence of nearly fourteen thousand people all holding their breath at the same time, as Will missed easy shots and fumbled the ball. Then he rallied, breaking Tanner's serve. But the Australian was too experienced to let that throw him. He powered through, breaking back in the next game. Unsettled, Will lost his serve on two double faults. The crowd groaned. Tanner rose to the challenge. He took the set.

Maddie sat despondently with her elbows on her knees. Will's game was falling apart. Ever since he had realised that James wasn't court-side, everything had gone wrong for him. The young player sat in the chair, head down, shoulders sagging.

Maddie looked at Danny. He was intent on his laptop. 'I'm going to go and look for James,' she said. 'I can't just sit here doing nothing.'

Danny glanced up at her. 'You be careful,' he said. 'Keep in touch. Your dad will go ballistic if anything happens to you.'

Maddie nodded. She made her way along the aisle. She climbed the steps and left the court. She knew that other PIC officers would already be looking for James, but she just couldn't sit there and watch Will's chance of winning ebb away. She had to do something.

✪

Danny's laptop was tuned to the TV again. In his ear, two BBC commentators debated what had gone wrong. From the dizzying heights of that first set, Will's game had gone into a slow, depressing, downward curve. He had lost the third set six-one. Then his luck had changed slightly. He had just managed to take the fourth set, capitalising on several uncharacteristic errors by the Australian.

The opinion of the TV commentators wasn't good. Will was playing poorly. If Craig Tanner kept his nerve and maintained his level of playing, Will would be in for an unpleasant fifth, and final, set.

✪

Maddie had been over the entire Wimbledon complex, searching through the crowds for any sign of James, speaking to every security guard and PIC officer she met.

'Have you seen James Anderson? Have you heard anything?'

No sightings. No information. Maddie braced herself to face the increasing possibility that Shadow had taken James instead. Then one of the security guards said that he had seen someone who looked like James walking into the restaurant on the Competitors' Terrace.

Maddie walked around to the Millennium Building on the west side of Centre Court. She entered and made her way up the stairs to the Competitors' Terrace. Her PIC pass got her through security. She crossed the terrace and went into the restaurant. This was exclusive territory. There were a few people in there, watching the final on a TV screen on one wall. James wasn't among them. Maddie walked the length of the restaurant and out the other end into a corridor. There were a few private offices along here.

She opened the first door and looked into a small, white room. James was sitting at a table. Hunched over. His head supported in his hands. The table was strewn with newspapers and magazines. He didn't look up.

'Hello, Maddie,' he said softly.

She stepped into the room, closed the door quietly behind her and walked over to the table. Will's face stared up from the table top a dozen times. All the magazines and newspapers were open at articles and pictures of James's successful brother.

'Is he winning?' James asked. The room was cool and quiet, with efficient air-con murmuring in the background.

'No.' Maddie sat down opposite James. She looked at him. Even at this short distance, it was impossible to tell that one of his eyes saw nothing. His gaze was fixed on the pictures of Will's face. He tapped the table with a pencil, agitatedly.

'James? What's wrong?' Maddie asked.

James's eyes rolled upwards to look into her face. He spoke very slowly. 'Do you know who I am, Maddie? I'm the guy with the blurry face in the back of all the pictures. That's all I am.' He laughed bleakly. 'The out-of-focus man.'

Maddie reached across the table and rested her hand on James's arm. 'That's not true,' she said, firmly but quietly. 'Will needs you. Come with me. Let's go out there together. Come on.'

James looked at her. He was trembling slightly. His face was clammy with sweat, in spite of the air-con.

'James?' Maddie whispered. 'What about it? Come with me?'

He didn't respond. He just sat there, staring at her with his one good eye and his one blind eye, and his long, angular face drained of colour.

Maddie felt her heart begin to beat faster. Suddenly the room felt suffocating. She had a dreadful suspicion that she was about to get out of her depth.

# Chapter Eighteen

The umpire's voice rang out over a subdued Centre Court: 'Game, Tanner. Tanner leads by five games to four, final set.'

More than once, Will had fought his way back from the very brink of disaster. Then, just as his supporters thought the tide of the match had turned, he would make a simple error that gave Craig Tanner the edge again.

And always, his eyes were darting up to the family seats – searching for a face that was never there. Alex understood the significance of those fleeting glances. He found James's absence disturbing too. James had been his usual self at breakfast in the rented apartment.

He and Will had discussed tactics. He had been there while Will was warming up in the screened-off practice courts.

Alex wracked his brains. Trying to pinpoint the moment when James had gone missing. Alex remembered talking to him on the way to the changing room. But then what? One minute he had been there with them, the next minute – gone.

Tanner delivered a blistering serve.

'Fifteen-love.'

Tanner was playing well. Will Anderson was playing badly. It was as simple as that. Alex turned to see how Johansson was coping with the imminent defeat of his client. The big Dane was leaning back in his seat, watching Will expressionlessly. It seemed to Alex as if the man was indifferent to Will's fate.

On court, Tanner scored an ace.

'Thirty-love.'

Groans went up from the audience.

The Australian threw the ball high. His racket snapped the air. The ball flashed over the net. It hit the ground smack on the line. A spurt of powder kicked up. Will hadn't even moved. The ball cracked against the backboard as if it had been fired from a gun.

'Forty-love.'

Three Championship points against Will Anderson.

Alex's eyes were drawn back to the game. Tanner prepared himself for the shot that would win the Championship. The crowded terraces of Centre Court fell silent.

The ball zipped over the net. Will whacked it back with a strong double backhand. Tanner lunged hard and managed to return it. Will charged for the net. He volleyed the ball hard and down. It bounced three times before Tanner could get near it.

An avalanche of applause broke out around the court.

From somewhere deep inside, Will had dredged up the spirit to fight back.

Three minutes later the two opponents were sitting on either side of the umpire's chair. The score was five games all.

Alex turned to look at Johansson. His face was as unreadable as a rock.

'Close thing,' Alex said to him.

Johansson nodded.

Alex frowned. He leaned closer. 'Why are you here, Lars?' he asked quietly. The unreadable eyes turned to him. Johansson didn't reply. Alex lowered his voice so that only the Dane could hear him. 'Why did you stay after you were told that there was no money?' he asked. 'It's been puzzling me. You don't owe Will anything. I don't think you even like him. So, why are you still here?' Alex's eyes narrowed. 'Am I missing something?' he whispered. 'Have you got some reason for wanting to be around Will – something that's more important to you than the money?'

The grey eyes hardened. The ghost of a smile cracked the Dane's lips. 'Yes,' he said. 'I do have a reason for being here that is more important to me than money.' The eyes flashed like splintered stone. 'A reason that is far more important to me.'

There was a wave of applause as the two opponents walked back on court.

Alex reached one hand into his pocket, feeling for his mobile. If his suspicions about Johansson were right, he was going to need backup.

✪

On the other side of the court, Danny could hardly watch the game.

'If that guy is trying to give me a heart attack, he's going the right way about it,' he muttered to himself. His eyes flickered from the screen of his laptop, up to the court, and back down again. The televised shot was a close-up of Will. He was sitting in his chair, staring straight ahead, as though lost in deep thought.

Danny looked at his watch. Maddie had been gone too long. He checked his earpiece was in place and opened a line to her on his laptop. A mobile phone chirruped close by. Danny looked down. Maddie's phone lay on her seat. Danny rolled his eyes. She'd gone off without it. *Great! Way to keep yourself safe, Maddie!*

He stared thoughtfully at the screen for a few moments. Then he closed the laptop down. He snapped it shut and slipped it into his soft leather briefcase. He took Maddie's mobile phone and dropped it into his pocket. She was going to get some serious verbal from him about that. This was not a good time for her to put herself out of communication. He stood up and edged his way along the row of seats. He climbed the stairs and went out through the exit.

Mission: find Maddie before she did something dumb.

Before she got herself into trouble.

✪

Alex watched Johansson carefully. There was a curious light in the Dane's eyes. Alex had the feeling that he was about to hear something that Lars Johannson had long kept to himself.

A secret? But what kind of secret?

'You ask me why I stay here to coach this boy?' Johansson murmured. He reached out and gripped Alex's wrist. 'I will tell you why I stay. I stay because I was once a boy like Will – a gifted boy – a boy with a great future.' He shook his head. 'But I knew I was talented, and I thought I could win without effort. I was wrong. It takes more than talent to win the Grand Slam tournaments. It takes hard work. This boy is like I was at his age. Too easily distracted.' Johansson stared into Alex's eyes, challenging and cold. 'With the right discipline, I could have been a champion. This boy will be a champion – and I will have done my duty.' He let go of Alex's wrist and leaned back, folding his arms. 'That is why I stay.' The face became impassive once more. 'I do not expect you to understand.' The grey eyes turned to the court.

Alex let out a long, relieved breath.

He took his hand off his mobile and turned to watch Will Anderson serve to stay in the match.

✪

Maddie and James faced one another across the table. Will's repeated images lay between them on the table top, gazing up at the ceiling from newspapers and magazines.

'Talk to me, James,' Maddie said softly.

He looked at her. She got the feeling he wasn't really seeing her.

'About what?' he asked. 'About Will? Everyone else is talking about Will – so why shouldn't we?' A sick smile lifted the corner of his mouth. 'What would you like to know about Will? I've got the inside story, Maddie. I can tell you things that no one else knows.'

Maddie looked steadily at him. Something suddenly fell into place. Something that had been nagging her for days. The newspaper photo. The tree. The three figures.

'How did the accident happen, James?' she asked. 'The accident when you hurt your eye.'

'I was in the house,' James said, his voice a dull monotone. It was as if he had reported his version of events a hundred times before. 'Will climbed the tree in our garden. He got scared. He couldn't get back down again. He shouted for help. There was no one else to help him. So I went to help him. I tried to talk him down but he was too scared. I climbed up after him. I tried to get him down. The branch broke and we fell. We fell into a neighbour's garden. We fell into her rose bush.' The smile appeared again. 'They were red roses. Will was knocked out on a stone. I got a thorn in my eye.'

His hand rose to cover his right eye. 'They operated on me, but it was no good. I lost the sight.' He moved his hand. 'You wouldn't know it, though, would you? To look at me, I mean? You wouldn't know I was half-blind.' His voice rose. 'You wouldn't know that it killed my chances of a career in tennis *stone dead*!' His hand clutched the pencil tightly, using the point to scratch at the magazine that lay in front of him.

Maddie took a deep breath. 'How did Will get up the tree?' she asked quietly. That was it! All along – that had been the thing about Mrs Greer's newspaper cutting that had puzzled her. It didn't make sense. Will had been alone in the garden. It was a tall tree. A tall tree with a long, smooth trunk. Maddie could see the photo in her mind. The lowest branches were above Mrs Greer's head. At a stretch, lanky eleven-year-old James might have been able to jump up and grab hold of the lowest branch. But not Will, seven years old and several inches shorter.

'I told you – he climbed up,' James said flatly.

'How?' Maddie asked. 'I've seen a picture of the tree, James. In the newspaper. I don't see how he could have got up the tree, not without help. The branches were too high.'

James didn't reply. He was staring at the tabletop,

concentrating on something that he was doing with the pencil. Twisting his wrist. Grinding the pencil point down into the magazine.

Maddie looked down at the magazines on the table.

Her heart began to pound.

James's hand moved up and down. Up and down. Sharp, hard, rapid movements that splintered the tip of the pencil.

James was stabbing the pencil into a photograph of Will.

He was stabbing Will's eyes.

# Chapter Nineteen

Maddie froze. Her heart seemed to lurch to a stop. She watched with horrible fascination as James drew another of the magazines across the table towards him. Again, the broken pencil was thrust knife-like down into the eyes. Blackening them. Tearing at them. Blinding them.

It was almost as if James had forgotten she was there. Then his eyes swivelled up and he stared at her. Smiling.

'It should have been me,' he said, his voice hoarse with emotion. 'It would have been me – out there – winning these matches. Getting all the attention. All the glory.'

Maddie's hand moved to her pocket. Feeling for her mobile phone. It wasn't there. She felt a wave of sickness. It must have fallen out of her pocket.

'It didn't really hit me until the American Open last summer,' James continued in the same unfamiliar voice. 'He ruined my life. If I hadn't gone up that tree to rescue him – if he hadn't made us fall – I'd be the one in all the newspapers.' His pencil gouged again and again. 'I'd be the one being photographed. I'd be the one on Centre Court right now.'

Maddie was terrified. It was as if a mask had slipped aside and something terrible had been revealed. She licked dry lips. Trying not to panic. Trying to keep her brain on the rails.

'I'm sorry,' she murmured. 'Truly, James, I'm so sorry. But...' She shifted her legs, balancing her weight on the balls of her feet. Preparing to get herself out of there. '...but it was just an accident. It wasn't Will's fault. It wasn't anyone's fault.' The legs of her chair scraped heavily against the thick carpet.

James stared at her.

Maddie swallowed. Show no fear, she told herself. 'I'm going to leave now, James,' she said calmly. She stood up, slowly, her eyes riveted to James's face.

James rose to his feet, his head still lowered, his eyes

still piercing her with that crazed look. He laughed. There was no humour in the sound. James slid a hand into a pocket. He drew out a mobile phone.

'Do you know what this is?' he asked.

Maddie stared at the mobile. She edged around the chair, gripping the back, ready to use it as a weapon if he came at her.

'Do you know what I've got here, Maddie?' James said. 'I've got revenge.'

He began to punch in a number, muttering the digits to himself under his breath. Maddie backed towards the door. Her hand groped behind her for the door handle. James looked up at her again.

'It's too late,' he said, smiling. 'I've done it. There's no going back now.'

Maddie's hand found the handle. She twisted it and pulled the door towards her. She moved to the side and slid through the gap. She slammed the door behind her and ran wildly along the corridor, her heart thundering and the blood pounding in her head.

○

'Game, Tanner. Six games all, final set.'

The crowd was going crazy. Will had held his own serve, and had come close to breaking the Australian's serve. Tanner had held on to his game with two blistering aces. The atmosphere in Centre Court crackled with tension. Despite drawing level, Tanner was beginning to look rattled. Will stood on the baseline and got ready to serve.

Somewhere in the middle of the crowd sat an unremarkable man. He wore smart, casual clothes – an open-necked polo shirt and well-cut cream trousers. His light-brown hair was short and neat. He had a soft, smooth face. He was wearing round, wire-rimmed shades. Blacked out.

He looked like a perfectly ordinary member of the Centre Court crowd – except for one thing. While the eyes of everyone around him swivelled back and forth with the yellow tennis ball, his eyes were fixed permanently on Will Anderson.

There was a silver case between his feet.

A series of chiming tones sounded from his pocket. His mobile phone. Programmed to play a refrain from Beethoven's Pastoral Symphony.

'I'm so sorry,' he murmured to his immediate neighbours. His voice was equally unremarkable, middle class and well-educated. 'I'm really so sorry about this.'

He took the phone out and pressed the OK button to stop the ringing. A text message appeared on the screen.

He put the phone away. He gripped the handle of the silver case.

The crowd roared as Will won his service game. Now all he had to do was break Tanner's serve to take the Championship.

The man took no notice.

'Excuse me,' he said, smiling apologetically as he stepped over his neighbours, bent double, heading for the end of the aisle. 'I'm sorry. Excuse me. Sorry. So sorry.'

He made his way up the steps towards the exit.

✪

Maddie ran into the restaurant and nearly collided with Danny.

He knew at once that something deadly serious had happened.

Maddie was breathless, her pale face still showing all the horror of her encounter with James.

'What?' he asked. 'Quick. What's happened?'

'It's James,' Maddie panted. 'He's sick. Crazy.' She gulped in air. 'I think James is Shadow. He's...' She waved her arm out behind her. She shook her head. There was no time to explain – no time for details. 'He sent a message on his mobile. I think he's made contact with Spider.'

Danny reacted instantly. He pulled out his mobile and pressed a preset button to open a line to Alex.

Alex answered on the first ring. 'Danny? What is it?'

'Shadow is *James*,' Danny said. 'Maddie's been with him. He's triggered Spider.'

'I'm on it.' The line went dead.

Danny looked at Maddie. 'We need to get James,' he said. 'You OK?'

Maddie nodded.

They ran out of the restaurant and back towards the white room.

❁

Alex was standing at one of the Centre Court exits, high under the canopy of roofing that shaded the upper tiers of seating. He was scanning the crowd through small binoculars. He was looking for something out of the ordinary. Something significant.

He had relayed Danny's message to Jack Cooper. The word had gone out. Spider was there. Spider had been triggered. Every PIC officer in the complex was racing towards Centre Court. Every exit was covered.

Alex felt the adrenaline pumping. They had to get to Spider before Spider got to Will. If that was possible. How long would it take for a professional hit man to fire a single, deadly bullet? A split second.

He'll have planned an escape route, Alex thought. Get the job done and get out undetected. That was Spider's MO. That's how he had avoided them for so long.

Alex raised his binoculars. The crowd wheeled in front of his eyes. At the back of the stadium, the walls were punctuated by the shaded windows of over forty TV and radio commentary boxes.

Alex wiped his sleeve across his forehead. He was sweating.

Gasps came from the simmering crowd. Applause. Shouting. Whistling. Craig Tanner had drawn level again.

A voice yelled from the crowd. 'Get on with it!' There was a ripple of uneasy laughter as the two men walked to their chairs beside the umpire.

Alex focused his binoculars on Will. He looked tired. He was mopping his face with a towel. He took a long swig from a plastic bottle. He peeled a banana and bit off a chunk. His eyes moved out across the court. He was still looking for James.

Alex was as tense as a bowstring. He dreaded at any second to hear the deadly crack of a sniper's rifle. He dreaded seeing Will slump forward in his seat, a red stain blossoming across his shoulder blades...

He would not let that happen. He gritted his teeth and continued his magnified search of the arena. There was no way that he was going to allow Spider to get to Will. No way in the world.

✪

The white room was empty. The magazines and newspapers were still there on the table. Mutilated. Danny glanced briefly at the pictures of Will with his eyes scratched out. He'd seen it before. But that didn't make it any less shocking.

Maddie pulled him back out of the room. She pointed towards the end of the corridor. An extendable metal ladder. An access hatch to the roof.

The hatch was open.

They ran. Maddie reached the ladder first. She climbed up, her feet pounding on each rung. Danny was right behind her.

'Be careful!' Danny yelled at her.

Maddie climbed out into bright daylight. She was on the high, curved roof of the Millennium Building. Behind her, she could hear the crowd-noises from Centre Court. To her right stretched the bulk of the building's long, grey roof. To her left, the southern courts. Ahead of her, the roof sloped gently down towards Somerset Road.

A figure crouched on the roof ahead of her, hunched up – like an animal at bay.

'James.'

He turned his eyes towards her. He didn't speak.

'You can't do this, James,' Maddie called. She lowered herself to his level. She knelt on the hot roof, feeling it hard through the knees of her jeans. 'I want to help you.'

James laughed.

'You can't let Will be killed!' Maddie burst out. 'You can't.'

James stared around, searching for another way down off the roof.

Maddie stood up. James was several metres away from her. The glare from the light-grey roof hurt her eyes. Her hands were slick with sweat.

She wiped her palms on her hips and began to walk unsteadily towards him.

# Chapter Twenty

The man with the silver case opened the door to one of the radio booths at the back of Centre Court. He stepped inside and silently closed the door. A woman sat at a small desk, speaking rapidly into a mike. She had her back to him, gazing through a wide, low window which overlooked the court. The man moved so quietly that the woman didn't even hear him. He stepped across the small booth and pulled out the mike's jack plug. As he did so he reached into his inside pocket with his right hand.

The woman turned in her chair, her face startled and angry. The man held a small handgun to the centre of her forehead. Her expression turned to one of sheer terror.

'I'm afraid you're going to be off-air for a few moments,' the man said, his voice soft. 'Please, don't be a hero.'

He lifted her from the chair, his left hand beneath her elbow. He steered her over to the corner and pushed her down on to her knees. Tucking his gun into the waistband of his trousers, he pulled a roll of tape from his pocket and gagged and bound her with swift, economical movements.

He dropped to one knee and laid his case flat on the floor. He opened the lid and lifted out a black rubber disc with a hand grip at the back. In his right hand, he held a diamond-tipped glass cutter. Standing up and reaching across the desk, he attached the rubber disc to the window, low in the right-hand corner. He scribed around the disc with the cutting tool. With a jerk, a circle of glass came away from the window. He looked through the hole. 'Excellent,' he said with quiet satisfaction.

He knelt again at the case and lifted out the sections of a Super Magnum sniper's rifle. He began to assemble them.

The woman watched him with terrified eyes. He paid no further attention to her. He had bound her securely, and she posed no threat to his operation.

It was stiflingly hot in the booth but the man wasn't sweating. Every few seconds, a burst of applause and cheering came rolling up. The match was under way again. The tennis players were obviously engaged in a gripping final battle.

The players. The Target and the other guy. He didn't know the other guy's name. It didn't concern him. He was utterly practical when it came to his work. He didn't waste time on irrelevant details.

The man took a small black device out of the case. He pressed buttons rapidly until a green light flashed. A slender black wire ran from the device to an earpiece, which he fitted into his ear.

He snapped a Laseraim AR-15 into place on top of the rifle and flicked a switch to activate the beam. He passed his hand in front of the sights. A small red dot appeared in his palm. He added a powerful CMO Marksman Elite scope, and a Brügger and Thomet high precision silencer at the end of the barrel. He smiled lovingly as he stroked the grey metal butt. It was a hand-crafted, finely-tooled instrument. A beautiful thing. Spider loved his gun.

He loved his work.

He stood up.

He was ready.

James stood up. He turned to face Maddie.

She was walking slowly towards him, her eyes fixed on his face. She looked scared.

The sound of applause drifted over from Centre Court.

James took a step backwards. He was close to the place where the roof began to slope down towards Somerset Road. Maddie paused. She lifted an arm and wiped the sweat out of her eyes. Her heart was pounding like a hammer. It was so stiflingly hot up there that she could hardly catch her breath.

'James!' she gasped, trying to keep eye contact. Contact with the living eye – not with the dead one. 'What did you do... when you used your... mobile?' She had to be sure. 'Who did you call?'

James stared at her. 'I told Spider to get the job done,' he said. He smiled. He looked elated, brittle. 'Do you know what it's like to be always in the shadows? It eats away at you, Maddie – it eats you alive.'

'You could get help,' Maddie said. 'You don't have to feel like this.'

James's head lowered. 'I couldn't take it any more,' he said hoarsely. 'I wanted to stop it – to stop *him* –

once and for all. To even the score between us. I had a plan. I tried to poison him. He didn't realise – he trusted me. He thought it was a tonic drink.' Demented laughter. 'That's why he lost his form, but he didn't know it, the stupid sap. He'd have been dead in six months if that fool Johansson hadn't interfered.'

'You wouldn't have done it, James,' Maddie said, struggling to keep her voice calm. 'You couldn't have killed him. He's your brother.' She swallowed hard. 'Is there any way to call Spider off?'

James didn't seem to have heard her. 'I haven't told you the best part,' he went on. He looked up at her, his eyes strained wide. 'I've given Spider very specific instructions. I've told him to shoot Will through his right eye.' He grinned. 'Poetic justice, get it? An eye for an eye. Isn't that perfect? Isn't that just completely perfect?'

Maddie stared at him. She was suddenly very afraid of him.

James was insane.

✪

Alex was standing by the spectators' exit. Negative reports kept coming into his earpiece from other PIC officers. No sightings so far. Nothing unusual. Spider had gone to ground.

This was bad.

Alex continued to search the court with his binoculars. Where was Spider? In the crowd? Down in the photographers' pits? Where?

A tumultuous roar erupted from the crowd. Something big had happened. Alex paused and looked down into the court. The umpire's voice floated up over the noise of the crowd.

'Love-forty.'

The score was seven-six to Will. Tanner was serving to stay in the match. Will had three Championship points.

The Australian threw the ball and lashed at it.

An ace – no question.

No! Somehow, Will had got to it. A flick of the wrist at full stretch.

The ball arched over the net. An easy shot for Tanner as he charged in. The ball whipped back at an impossible angle. Will threw himself across the court. He clipped the ball and it sliced back over the net. Tanner made a suicidal dive. He managed to tag the ball, but it went high.

There was a great collective gasp from the crowd as the ball sailed upwards. It lost momentum. It curved. It began to fall.

Will was there. He jumped, smashing the ball down over the net with all his strength.

Tanner didn't stand a chance.

The audience went crazy.

Will had won.

Alex's eyes narrowed. He tore himself away from the jubilant scene. Will Anderson was the new Wimbledon Men's Champion – and he was about to get shot.

✪

Foam flecked the corners of James's mouth. He was babbling now. Maddie could hardly understand a word that he was saying. He was talking about the accident. Blaming Will. Pouring out ten years' worth of pent-up anger and bitterness, harboured resentments that had festered and gone rotten inside him. Dark emotions that had short-circuited his mind.

'James!' Maddie shouted against his incoherent ranting. 'Listen to me! How did Will get up the tree, James? How did he do it? *Why* did he do it? He was afraid of heights. Why would he climb up the tree on his own?'

James became silent. The smile was gone. His face looked uninhabited.

'He was such a scaredy-cat about that tree,' he said. His voice had a childish, singsong rhythm. 'I used to laugh at him, but he wouldn't climb it. Not unless I made him.'

'You were in the garden with him, weren't you?' Maddie said quietly. 'You made him go up the tree. And then he got frightened, and you had to climb up to help him. And that was when you fell. That's how it happened, isn't it?'

An explosion of cheering came across the rooftop of the Millennium Building, like the roaring of a storm-tossed sea. A tumult of applause from Centre Court. James's eyes widened, showing white all round. His mouth fell slack.

'He's won...' he gasped. He grimaced as if in agony. His voice was a ragged shout. 'He won – without me. He won!'

✖

Will leaped the net like a gazelle, buoyed by the uproarious cheering of the crowd. He was laughing. Waving his arms triumphantly in the air. He hugged Craig Tanner. The Australian slapped him on the back. It was a well-deserved victory.

No one noticed the tiny red point of light that pirouetted on the back of Will's white shirt.

The man was leaning across the desk in the commentary booth. The long barrel of the rifle was pointing out through the hole in the glass, down into the court. The expensive sunglasses lay on the desk beside him. His head was cocked. One eye to the sight. One eye closed. His finger was on the trigger. He was smiling in anticipation of a job well done.

He was waiting for the perfect moment. He had his instructions. A single shot through the right eye. Tricky at that distance. Tricky, but not impossible. Not for a professional.

Will Anderson just needed to turn around.

The finger squeezed the trigger.

✪

Alex's heart crashed against his ribcage like a hammer. He had spotted something through his binoculars. Way over on the far side of the court, under the roof. A glint of light on metal. Light glinting on a rod of dark metal where there should be no rod of dark metal. It was jutting out from a black hole in one of the windows of a commentary box. Alex recognised the deadly shape. It was the barrel of a rifle.

He took his mobile out of his pocket and pressed a single number.

'Cooper.' The Chief Superintendent's voice barked sharply in his earpiece.

Alex lowered his head to the transceiver so he could be heard above the noise of the crowd.

'I have him,' he said quietly. He gave brief, precise details.

'OK,' came Cooper's voice. 'Do nothing, Alex. I'm sending in the heavy boys.'

The heavy boys – armed Special Branch officers. Alex let out a breath. He'd done it. He was one hundred per cent certain that he had pinpointed Spider's position. Now all he had to do was to wait. Special Branch would take Spider out. Alex never found waiting easy. It was hard to stand back and let other people finish the job.

He lifted the binoculars to his eyes again. He zoomed in on the window with the ring of missing glass. The rifle barrel was still there – but the angle had changed since he had last looked. It was aimed higher.

Alex didn't notice the small red spot that suddenly appeared on his shirt front. It wandered for a few moments before coming to rest over his heart.

His thundering heart.

✪

Danny had his head up through the roof hatch. He was keeping a low profile, giving Maddie a chance to talk James down. She wasn't having much luck. Things were bad up there.

James looked like he was about to blow.

Danny hauled himself up, his shoulders clearing the hatch. Sweat ran out of his hair and dripped down his face. He didn't like the way the roof sloped away: the closer to the edge, the steeper the curve. James had moved out on to the slope – and Maddie was perilously close. One wrong move and either of them could lose their footing. And then it would be a helpless slide down to the roof edge. Over the edge. Fifteen metres down on to concrete.

Slam!

A killing drop.

✪

James stared into Maddie's face.

'I made him go up the tree,' he said slowly. He put his hand up over his right eye. 'I forced him up there. It was all my fault – not Will at all – it was me. *My* fault.'

'It was an *accident*,' Maddie said. She took a step towards him. She felt the curve of the roof under her foot. It was smooth. Slippery.

'My fault.' James's voice was dull. Dead. 'My fault all the time.'

Maddie took another step. Her heel slid under her. She almost lost balance. She tried to keep her voice controlled. 'No! No one's fault. *Listen* to me, James.'

'I've killed him!' James shouted, his eyes wild.

Something seemed to snap in his mind. Maddie saw it clearly in the agony that spread grotesquely across his face. He backed away from her. His arms windmilled as he tried to keep his footing on the roof. His feet slipped out from under him. He toppled backwards and began to slide inexorably down the curve of the roof.

Maddie threw herself forwards with a cry. Their fingers touched for a moment before he slithered away from her. She scrambled forwards, ignoring her own peril. There was less than a metre between them.

'James!' she screamed, reaching frantically out to him.

His arms stretched out towards her. She flung herself full length on the burning roof. Winded, red flames rimmed her vision. She caught his groping hand. His feet were out over empty air and a terrible drop.

Maddie let out a cry of horror. She was sliding with him. She tried to dig her toes in, to gain some hold on the slick roof. It was no good. James's weight was pulling her down. Sweat blinded her. There was an insane screaming in her ears. Her head was swimming. She had a stark choice. A terrible choice.

Either she let go of James, or she went with him.

That was it.

Either she let him die – or they both died.

# Chapter Twenty-One

The Super Magnum bolt-action sniper rifle fires high power .338 calibre Lapua bullets. It is deadly accurate up to eleven hundred metres.

The man smiled faintly as the red laser dot came to rest on Alex's chest. He had heard Alex's transmission from Jack Cooper. It had come through loud and clear in his earpiece. The small black device from his case had been specifically designed to monitor localised transmissions.

A lesser man might have aborted the job on learning that the police were breathing down his neck. But not Spider. The police officer called Alex, and all the other cops that Spider now knew were on his trail – they didn't change a thing. Spider had a reputation to live up to. He had never failed a client yet. He was not about to start now. He was Number One.

The ammunition clip held five bullets: one for the young police officer named Alex, one for Will Anderson. That left three bullets and his handgun for anyone else who got in his way. More than enough to secure his safe exit.

Spider's finger tightened on the trigger.

❂

Maddie let out a wordless scream as she felt herself being dragged down the slope of the roof. She couldn't let go of James. She couldn't let him fall to his death. The roof seemed to lurch under her. The hot metal burned her cheek. The sky reeled. She felt powerless. Terrified.

Something strong and firm clamped around her ankles, stapling her to the roof.

'Hold on, Maddie!' Danny's voice was close behind her. He had seen James fall. He had seen Maddie throw herself after him. As he watched her slide away, clinging to James, he hurled himself recklessly through the hatch.

Danny stretched out further and grabbed Maddie's belt. He tried to drag her to safety, but James's dead weight was too much for him.

'James!' Danny panted. 'Help me out!'

James lay spread-eagled on the roof. His head was down, his legs dangling loose over the long fall to the ground.

'Don't you give up now, mate!' Danny gasped. 'Maddie? You OK?'

'Yes.' Her hair dripped sweat into her eyes. Stinging.

Danny crawled along her body and reached for James. He grabbed hold of his sleeve.

'OK. Pull!'

Together, they managed to drag the limp form up the roof towards the hatch. James made no sound as they hauled him across the scorching metal.

Danny went down the ladder. Maddie manoeuvred James around on the roof and guided his legs through the hatch. As James's legs appeared, Danny grabbed him. He backed slowly down the ladder, James heavy against him. James slumped to the floor in Danny's arms. Maddie scrambled down the ladder. Trembling and panting.

James's eyes opened. 'What have I done?' he whispered, his eyes staring and unfocused. 'What have I done to Will?'

Maddie knelt at his side. 'Can you call Spider off?' she asked urgently.

Two empty eyes turned to her. 'Yes.'

'How? With the mobile?'

'Yes.'

Maddie searched his pockets. She found his mobile and held it under his face. 'Do it!' she urged.

James pulled himself into a sitting position. He wiped his sleeve across his face. With painful slowness he started to enter a text message. He pressed Send. He looked at Maddie, his face full of desperate misery.

She smiled and took hold of his hand. 'It's OK,' she said gently. 'Everything's OK now.'

James's face crumpled. He began to sob.

❋

The red point of light steadied over Alex's heart. Spider's finger was tightening on the trigger. Alex had only a split second to live.

Spider's mobile bleeped. His finger relaxed. Without moving the laser dot from Alex's shirt-front, Spider reached for his mobile and opened the line.

A text message.

EYES TIGHT SHUT

Spider's eyebrows raised slightly. He smiled ruefully and clicked his tongue.

He pulled his rifle back from the hole in the window. He slipped down on to one knee and began slowly and methodically to dismantle the rifle. He fitted the pieces neatly, one by one, into the silver case.

❂

Alex had a problem. He couldn't see the rifle barrel any more through his binoculars. He couldn't tell if Spider was still there. What if the gunman had moved? What if that rifle was now pointing at Will from some other place?

Alex took a long breath. His orders were to leave it to Special Branch. He hesitated. He was unarmed. It would be crazy to go anywhere near the assassin. He knew that. He couldn't just stand there doing nothing. Every instinct was telling him to get over there.

He began to run round the long walkway to the other side of the court, pushing his way through the spectators who had begun to drift towards the exits. Alex counted doors until he came to the right booth. The door was open. Pressing himself against the wall, he slid closer to the open doorway, every sense alert, every muscle tensed and ready.

There was something on the floor, just outside the door – a mobile phone.

He crouched down and picked it up. There was a text message. Unsent.

HELLO ALEX. NEXT TIME YOU'RE DEAD.

Alex felt sick.

✪

New instructions were coming in from Jack Cooper. All PIC units to report to Control in the Met Office by Centre Court. Immediately. Two security guards were down. Unconscious from blows to the head but not fatally injured. A car had been hijacked and driven away at speed.

The man had made his escape.

✪

Maddie stayed with James while Danny went to get help. She knelt at his side. Holding his hand. He lay there in absolute silence, staring at nothing, his face a horrible blank. She looked up when she heard Danny coming along the corridor with the paramedics.

They lifted James on to a stretcher-chair and covered him with a blanket. He clung to Maddie's hand as they wheeled him through the restaurant, down the stairs and out to where the ambulance was waiting.

Maddie watched the ambulance drive away. She could still feel the desperate, clammy grip of James's hand. She could still see the lost, helpless look on his face. She felt drained. Exhausted.

Danny stood next to her. 'You OK?'

She looked at him. 'No.'

They saw Alex walking towards them. His face was pale.

'Spider got away,' he said. 'But we got close. Baxendale's confident she'll get him next time.'

An amplified voice drifted over the high wall of the Centre Court building.

Will's voice.

He was being presented with the famous trophy.

'... and I'd like to thank my brother James – wherever he is right now – I'd like to thank him for all his love and support over the years. I wouldn't he holding this cup right now if it wasn't for him. Thanks for everything, James!'

The three exhausted PIC colleagues looked at one another. There was nothing to say.

# Chapter Twenty-Two

Will Anderson sat quietly and alone in a small office in the Millennium Building. He had asked for a few minutes of privacy. He was gathering himself for the second great challenge of the day: the live press conference. He was sitting with his arms loose across his knees, his head hanging. His mind spinning.

Wimbledon Champion.

Winner of the Men's Singles Final.

Earlier in the week, he had visited the Wimbledon Museum. He had gazed at all those famous names and faces from the past. It hadn't seemed possible that he could ever be added to their ranks. It still didn't. Even now. It hadn't really sunk in yet.

The euphoria of victory had quickly burned away – now he just felt empty and alone. Very alone. Where was his brother? James had not been at Centre Court. In all the turmoil of congratulations that had followed the match, Will only had one thought in his head: where was James? His victory felt hollow if he couldn't share it with his brother. No one knew where James was. No one would tell him. Will felt as if he was surrounded by people who were conspiring to keep something from him.

There was a soft knock on the door. Will looked up, suddenly filled with hope.

'James?'

The door opened.

✪

Two minutes earlier.

The corridor – outside that same office.

Maddie, Alex and Danny. With a problem.

'Someone's got to tell him,' Alex said. 'Everyone knows about James except him.' He jerked his head towards the door. 'Do you want some reporter to blurt it out in front of live TV cameras? Is that the way for him to find out?' Alex altered the tone of his voice slightly, in imitation of a braying press reporter. 'Your brother has just been taken to hospital, Will. Rumours are, he's gone whacko – would you like to tell us how you feel about that?' Alex looked at his two companions. 'We can't let that happen.'

'Don't look at me,' Danny said, raising his hands. 'I can't tell him. No way.'

Alex shook his head. 'I wouldn't know what to say. How do you tell a guy who's just won Wimbledon that his own brother's been trying to kill him for the last six months?'

Danny frowned. 'You don't tell him the whole story, that's for sure,' he said. 'He'd freak! He only needs to know that James has been taken to hospital. He doesn't need to be told every last little detail right now.'

Maddie had been quiet. Lost in thought. 'Yes, he does,' she said softly. 'He needs to know that James is ill.' She looked at them. 'He needs to know that James has been suffering from some kind of mental illness. He needs proper help, and he'll get it now. The person who hired Spider to shoot Will wasn't the real James. I saw that when we were up on the roof. I saw the real James there for a few moments – the James who realised what he'd done.' She shivered at the memory. 'I'll never forget the look on his face.'

'The guy's going to be in therapy for the longest time,' Danny said quietly.

Maddie nodded.

'Will is going to be torn apart by this,' Alex said. 'It's going to destroy him.'

'No, it isn't,' Maddie contradicted. 'You'd be surprised what people can live through.' Her eyes shone with a resolute light. 'I'm going to tell him,' she said firmly. 'Right now.'

Danny reached out a cautionary hand, but let it fall again when he saw the determination in her face.

Maddie stood in front of the door. She took a couple of long, slow breaths. Then she knocked. She opened the door and stepped into the room. The door closed quietly behind her.

Danny and Alex stood facing each other in the corridor.

'Know something?' Danny said. 'She's the bravest one of all of us.'

✪

The look of elation faded from Will's face. It wasn't James who slipped through the door. It was Maddie Cooper. She closed the door. She stood there for a few moments, looking at him. There was something in her face that scared him. Sorrow and sympathy and a deep compassion.

'It's James, isn't it?' he said.

Maddie nodded. 'Yes,' she said. 'It's James.'

His voice shook. 'Tell me.'

She walked across the room towards him.

The next few minutes felt like the most difficult of her life.

✪

The Millennium Building Press Room.

Seats rose in curved tiers from the long table.

The place was packed out. Media reps from all over the world were waiting hungrily. Will sat at the table, flanked by Wimbledon officials and by Lars Johannson. For once, the sober-faced Dane was smiling. As Danny observed, there's a first time for everything.

Danny and Alex stood at the back, on the highest tier. Keeping out of the way. From up there, Will looked young and vulnerable.

The new men's champion was coping masterfully with the press conference.

Alex whispered in Danny's ear. 'He's doing really well. You'd never believe what he's just found out.'

Danny nodded. 'Tell me about it.'

They hadn't seen Maddie since she had gone into the room to tell Will about James. They had expected her to be at the conference. But Will had entered alone, his face calm and unreadable.

Now he faced the question that Alex and Danny had been dreading.

'Can you tell us anything about what is wrong with your brother? Is it true that he's been taken to hospital?'

A shadow of sorrow passed over Will's face, but his voice was clear and steady as he replied. 'All I want to say right now is that I owe my entire career to James. If it wasn't for him, I wouldn't be here now. As soon as this conference is over, I'll be going to him. It's my intention to do everything I can to help my brother get well again. That is my absolute priority.' He lifted a hand against the rising tide of questions. 'That is all I'm prepared to say right now. I'll take questions on other subjects.'

Danny and Alex looked at one another.

Impressed.

❂

Maddie stood on the grassed rooftop terrace of the Broadcast Centre. She leaned on the rail, gazing out over the northern courts – the milling crowds, the high, round walls of No. 1 Court, the Aorangi Picnic Terrace. She felt very low. Emotionally drained. Her long talk with Will had taken a lot out of her. And it had reminded her of the tragedy that had so changed her own life, less than one short year ago.

'Strawberries and cream, miss?'

She looked around. Danny and Alex were standing behind her. Danny was holding out a white polystyrene tub. She took it with a faint smile.

'Thanks.'

'You took some finding, girl,' Danny said. 'We thought you'd gone into hiding.'

'I wanted to think,' Maddie said.

'Are you done thinking now?' Danny asked. He smiled.

Maddie laughed. 'Yes.'

'We've been at the press conference,' Alex said.

'How did he do?'

'Brilliantly,' Danny said. 'He walked it like a pro.'

Alex looked closely at her. 'How did he take it?' he asked. 'Did you tell him everything?'

Maddie nodded. 'He felt sorry for James,' she said. Her voice felt thick with emotion. 'That was his first reaction – he felt sorry for him. He said he should have realised how bad James had been feeling all those years. He blamed himself for not understanding how hard it must have been for him.' She looked from Danny to Alex. 'Can you believe that?'

'I guess James is all the close family Will's got left,' Danny said.

'He said he's going to do everything he can to make sure James gets better,' Maddie went on. 'He's an amazing guy.'

Alex looked at her and smiled. 'You're pretty amazing yourself, Maddie,' he said. 'I couldn't have done what you did. I couldn't have told him about James.'

Maddie smiled back. 'We all did our bit today. It was teamwork. That's how come we won – game, set and match.'